The Bowdoin Report Card

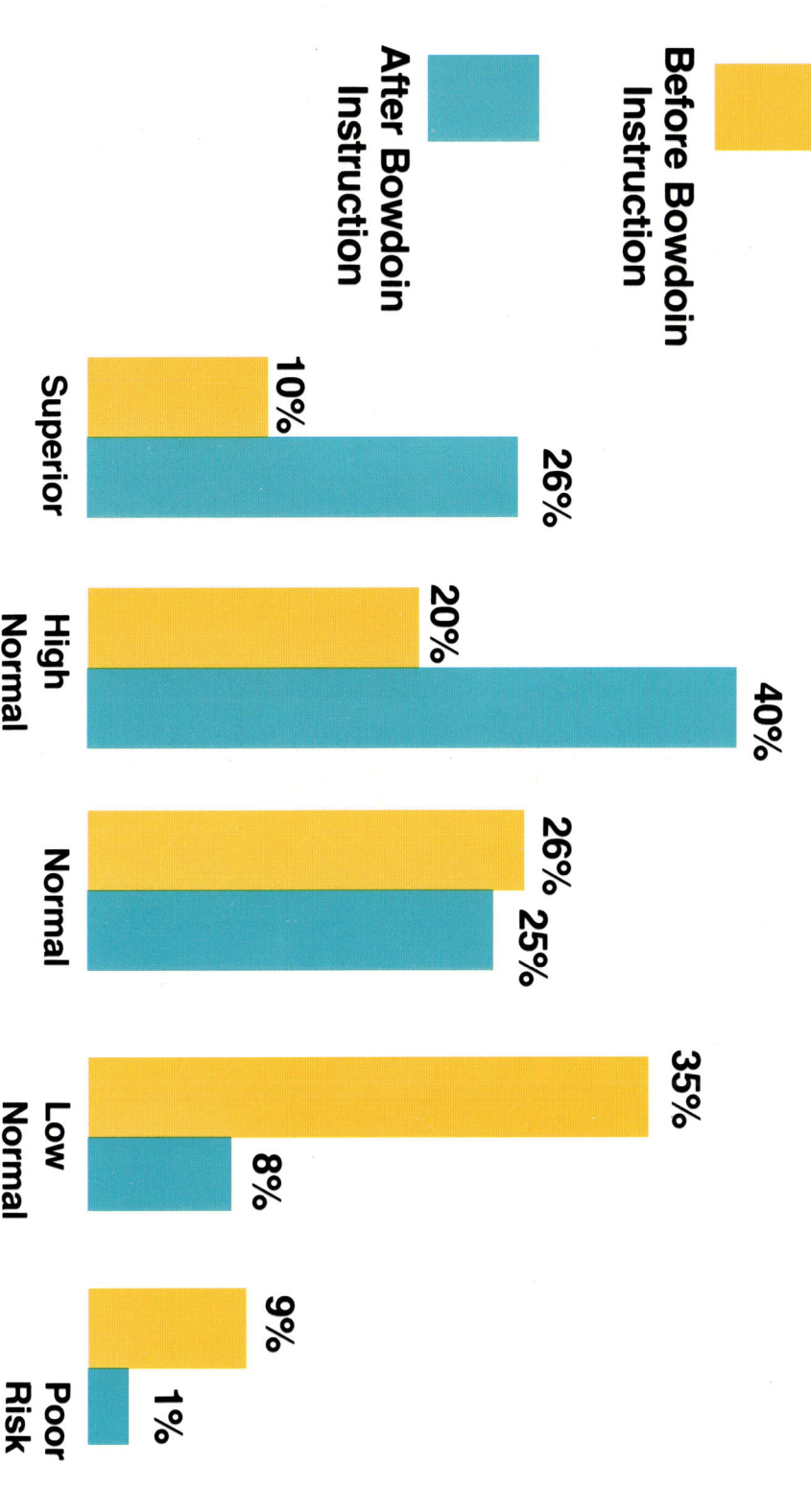

■ Before Bowdoin Instruction
■ After Bowdoin Instruction

Superior	10% / 26%
High Normal	20% / 40%
Normal	26% / 25%
Low Normal	35% / 8%
Poor Risk	9% / 1%

This graph depicts the statistically significant increases in the academic achievement of the school population in which Ruth Bowdoin developed her parent education method. The Metropolitan Readiness Test (a national standardized test) was used to measure the changes brought about by using the concepts and methods taught in the Bowdoin books for parents.

THE MAGICAL YEARS

The Bowdoin Method at Home

© 1989 The Southwestern Company, Nashville, Tennessee
Original Copyright 1976 by Webster's International Tutoring Systems, Inc.
Published with special permission from Webster's International.

Introduction

THE MAGICAL YEARS — The Bowdoin Method at Home

In the mid-sixties, Ruth Bowdoin saw the handwriting on the wall: Problem children would soon outnumber normal in our schools unless something dramatic could be done to improve the child's self-concept and learning abilities.

So, she began doing something dramatic. She began preparing materials that would involve the parent, at home, with the child. ("After all," she says, "the parent is the best teacher.") She very carefully avoided institutional language in her lessons, writing simply, directly, clearly. ("So many of the parents want to do the best thing, but don't know how.")

In testing and employing her methods, Ruth Bowdoin created her now-famous "Classroom on Wheels," in which parents and children were brought together — on location — to share the learning experience.

The results? After an evaluation of 3000 projects, the United States Office of Education selected only eight for national dissemination. One of those was the Bowdoin project. The next year, Ruth Bowdoin's methods won the coveted "Educational Pacesetter Award."

About the Author:
RUTH BOWDOIN ("BOW-den")

Ruth Bowdoin has been an Educator for 35 years. She has won the Educational Pacesetter Award for contributions to experimentation, creativity, and innovation in education. She also has won the Merit Award—Western States Exposition, and has been honored in a special resolution by the Tennessee State Board of Education. She is listed in "The Women's Who's Who in the World," "Who's Who in America—Early Childhood Edition" and "Personalities in the South."

TABLE OF CONTENTS

Chapter 1 . . . HOW TO TEACH YOUR CHILD AT HOME 5

Chapter 2 . . . HOW TO HELP YOUR CHILD DEVELOP
PRE-READING SKILLS 53

Chapter 3 . . . HOW TO TEACH YOUR CHILD WORD MEANINGS 89

Chapter 4 . . . HOW TO HELP YOUR CHILD DEVELOP EMOTIONALLY 117

Chapter 5 . . . HOW TO DEVELOP YOUR CHILD'S SELF ESTEEM 141

Chapter 6 . . . HOW TO CONTROL YOUR CHILD WITH GOOD WORDS 169

Chapter 7 . . . HOW TO MANAGE YOUR CHILD FOR GOOD BEHAVIOR 205

Chapter 1
HOW TO TEACH YOUR CHILD AT HOME

Dear Parent:

The lessons in this book have been designed to be used by teachers, paraprofessionals, tutors, home visitors, and parents, or other family members. Before a child learns to read, many things are needed which will help develop the skills, attitudes, and understandings that provide early success in reading. None of these lessons requires any special materials — they are all available in every home and are designed to focus on the development of things our young children need to know before formal reading instruction is begun:

1. **WORD MEANINGS AND UNDERSTANDINGS** (Usually the child who speaks many words well has a better chance to learn to read.)
2. **VISUAL DISCRIMINATION** (Recognizing likenesses and differences, looking, observing.)
3. **CATEGORIZING** (Finding things that belong to or do not belong to a group.) This is thinking!
4. **AUDITORY** (Listening for sounds, listening to you as you talk and read, following directions.)
5. **TACTILE** (Feeling things.)

Keep this book safe from little hands. Use it many times; children learn much by repetition. There are many other things that you can think of which you can do with your child that are similar to the lessons in this book. Nature is a whole world of learning! Teach your child to observe; and encourage questions, and develop curiosity.

Make your lessons fun! Make them short (ten minutes is plenty long).

REMEMBER, PARENTS, YOU ARE A TEACHER, AND THE MOST IMPORTANT TEACHER YOUR CHILD WILL EVER HAVE.

Happy Teaching!

Ruth Bowdoin

Lesson 1

Fun With Sandwiches

What You Need: Two pieces of bread and something for a sandwich (such as peanut butter, jelly).

Why: To teach number understandings, shapes, and many word meanings.

What You Do: As you prepare your child something to eat, or cook dinner for your family, talk and teach your little one!

Suppose you are making a sandwich — carry on a conversation such as:

"How many *pieces of bread* will we need?"

"What *else* will we need?" (Encourage your child to tell you — a *knife* for *spreading*, jelly, peanut butter, etc.)

"How *much* do we have left in the jar?" (Encourage your child to *see* if it is *about empty, almost full, half full.*) If it is about gone, say, "Yes, we have just about eaten it all. We will soon have to *buy some more.*"

When you are spreading the peanut butter, tell your child what you are doing:

"I *spread* the peanut butter to *this corner,* now to *another corner,* and now I'll turn it around to the other two corners."

"How many corners do we have? Count with me. One, two, three, four! Yes . . . this is called a *square* . . . say it with me. Yes, a square." (You are teaching shapes and numbers.)

"Now, we'll put the other piece on top. Would you like to have it cut into *two pieces,* or do you want it *whole*?" (Mother, you are teaching numbers which will help your child later . . . and you are giving him a choice.) If he says in two pieces, say, "Now I'll take my knife and cut from one corner to another corner . . . look, I've made a *triangle* . . . it has *three* sides. Count them with me."

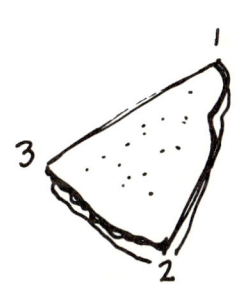

"Now are you *ready* to eat? Remember, *careful,* don't drop crumbs . . . That's a good boy (or girl). My, isn't it delicious? It is very good."

Mother, this is a sample of how you may talk to your little one as you work. It shouldn't take any more of your time. Your child will be happy that you are talking. He will learn many words!

A simple sandwich can help you teach 25 or more word meanings! But your child will not learn the first time . . . keep repeating!

THE BOWDOIN METHOD

Lesson 2

Teaching With Potatoes

What You Need: One or more potatoes.

Why: Word meanings, number relationships, understandings.

What You Do: If you are opening a new sack of potatoes such as you see here, there are many things you may do which will be learning for your little one:

1. Talk about *opening* or *untying* the *bag* or the *sack*.

2. Ask your child, "Are there *many* potatoes or a *few* in the sack?" (Explain what these words mean... he will need to know in school.) Always compliment when he tells you.

3. "Let's see, I think I'll need six potatoes... count with me and take them out for me." (You count and let him count after you.)

4. "Now I am going to *prepare* some for *supper*. How will I get them *ready*?" (Encourage your child to tell you.) Use the words *peel, mash, cook, boil, knife, soft, salt, water,* and any other words which come naturally with your cooking.

When there is time after your work, take one potato — talk about the *outside* and the *inside*. Show your child how they look different. (Teach the words alike and different.) Show your child the *eyes* of the potato and tell him that when the farmer plants potatoes he cuts the potato so that the "eye" will *grow under the ground* and come up and make a *plant*. Then little potatoes will grow around the roots under the ground and get *bigger* and bigger. Then the *farmer digs* them and *brings* them to the *store* (the *market*) and we *buy* them to eat!

(Your child may not understand all you say... but you would be surprised how much he may remember.)

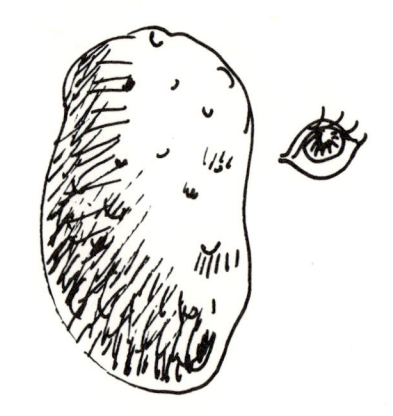

After you have talked about the "eyes of the potato," let him show you his eyes. "What do you do with your eyes? Yes, you see, you look. Can a potato see?" (Brag on him when he says, "No".)

Remember you are teaching your child how to think!

5. Take three potatoes, one small, one middle sized, one larger.

Ask your child to show you the *biggest* one, the *next biggest* and the *smallest* (least). Show him... and then ask him again.

Remember... PRAISE YOUR CHILD!

When there is time, show your child how to make a face from a potato by scooping out the eyes, nose, mouth. Let him show you while you do the work. Use string or rags for the hair. This will be fun! You could cook the "potato man" later!

Mother: Do this lesson several times during the year! Your child will learn *30* or more word meanings. How important this is!

Lesson 3

An Apple A Day...

What You Need: An apple.
Why: To teach your child new words and develop new understandings.

What You Do: Talk to your child about the apple.

What *shape* is it? (Talk about its being *round*.) What *color* is the apple? (Repeat what the child says, except you say a complete sentence, "Yes, the apple is red.") Is an apple a *fruit* or a *vegetable*? (Explain that it is a fruit. Name other fruits, and name some vegetables.)

Is it a *whole* apple or a *part* of an apple? (You are teaching your child number concepts that he will need in school.)

Tell your child about where apples come from. Talk about *climbing* a *ladder* and *picking apples* from a *big, tall tree*. Talk about *putting* them in a *basket*—picking a *bushel*.

Talk about *raw* apples and *cooked* apples.

Take a knife. Cut the apple in *two halves*. Talk about two *halves* being a *whole*. Then cut the halves into *fourths*. Let your child *count the pieces*.

Show your child the *seeds*. Talk about the seeds being *dark*. Count the seeds. Tell your child that seeds, when *planted* in the *ground*, *grow* to be a tree. It will come up and get bigger and bigger and bigger and will make apples.

Peel one of the fourths of the apple. Talk about what you are doing. Talk about the *inside* and the *outside* and the *difference* in color.

Let your child eat the apple. Talk about its being *sweet, juicy, delicious, good!*

Let your child *pretend* to have *apples for sale*.

Apples, apples!
Come buy apples!
Red, juicy apples!
Apples for sale!

Say this several times. Let your child pretend to put some apples in a sack for you. Tell him you wish to buy a *dozen* . . . or a *half dozen*. Help him count as he puts them in a sack.

You pretend to *pay him cash* for them.

(All children this age like "make-believe" and they learn from it!)

Give your child a color crayon and let him make some apples. Be sure to compliment him!

THE BOWDOIN METHOD

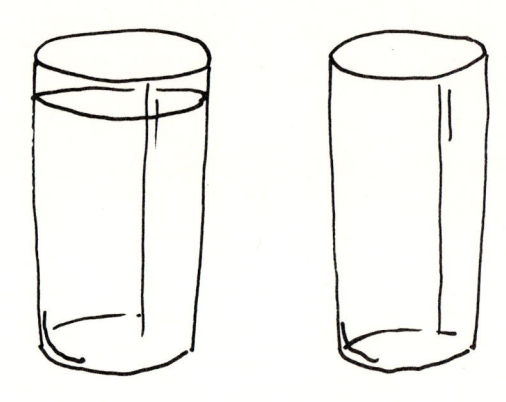

Lesson 4

Full Glass, Empty Glass

What You Need: Several glasses from the kitchen.

Why: To teach children to think, to develop understandings, and likenesses and differences. To teach *full* and *empty and other number relationships.*

What You Do: Fill one glass *full* of water. Have another *empty* one. Talk about what these mean.

Tell your child to "empty one glass." (Show what you mean.)

Have two glasses ½ *full* of water and one glass empty. Show your child how to fill the empty glass by pouring the two glasses that are ½ full into the empty one. Show how you *pour* water without *spilling*.

Count the glasses with your child.
Teaching other understandings
Ask: Why do we use glasses?
   What can *we drink* from a glass? (Encourage your child to think of milk, water, juice, soft drinks, etc.)
   What color is milk? Orange juice? Chocolate milk?
   Why must we be careful with a glass? (Explain that it will break when dropped.)

Place three glasses of different sizes on the table. Say:

Find the glass Mother would use.
Find the glass baby would use.
Find the glass you would use.
(Help your child understand that big people need larger glasses.)

Teaching Likenesses and Differences
Place 2 little glasses, 2 big glasses on the table (mixed up). Have your child find: two big ones; two little ones.

Place 3 glasses *alike,* one *different*

(in size or color) on the table. Tell your child to *find* the one that is different. Compliment your child for correct responses!

CHANTING (Children learn by chanting . . . they enjoy it also.)

Chant this with your child and teach him how to act it out and say with you.
Drink! Drink!
I drink milk.
(Pretend to drink.)
Good! Good!
Milk is good.
(Smack your lips.)
Full! Full!
I'm so full!
(Rub stomach.)
Strong! Strong!
I'll grow strong!
(Show arm muscle.)
Big! Big!
I'll grow big!
(Stand tall.)

THE BOWDOIN METHOD

Lesson 5

Learning And Cooking

What You Need: Things in the kitchen you might use when you are cooking.

Why: To teach number understandings, action words, and other word meanings.

What You Do: Mother, this is a sample lesson which you might do when cooking *anything* from bacon to biscuits, pie, cake, or vegetables.)

Could you let your little one stand on a chair and watch you as you do a job in the kitchen? What fun it will be as your child talks and asks questions while you work . . . and how much learning can take place!

You could do these things:

1. "I think I'll make a pie. What kind of pie could we make?" If your child does not know chocolate, chess, etc., begin to talk about the different kinds . . . and if you plan to make "chocolate," let him think he is helping you decide. (It is good for children to have a part in making decisions . . . then they think they are important! They feel that you respect their feelings . . . it will help them in choices later.)

"Let's see what we need." All this time you are getting out the things you need . . . naming them as you do and letting him name them after you. (He is learning the names of flour, sugar, cocoa, cup, rolling pin, bowl, crust, milk, vanilla, butter, etc.)

2. He will be learning some *arithmetic* if you talk about:

measuring the flour
one cup of sugar
two tablespoons of margarine
three eggs
baking for *30 minutes*
(Show the difference in the sizes of the two spoons.)

3. Your child will learn the meaning of *many action words* if you talk about: *breaking* the eggs, *putting* them in a bowl, *beating the ingredients together,* rolling *the pastry,* cutting the pastry to fit the pie pan, *putting* the pie in the oven to *bake, watching* it, *taking* it out of the oven!

4. Children like rhythm . . . they like made-up songs . . . they like pretend.

When rolling the dough, say: "We roll, roll, roll the dough, dough, dough!" (Let your child say it too . . . *watch your child smile.*)

"We cut, cut, cut, with our knife, knife, knife!"

"We beat, beat, beat . . . we beat the eggs!"

Sing to the tune of "Here we go round the mulberry bush." "This is the way we bake our pie, bake our pie, bake our pie. This is the way we bake our pie so early in the morning."

THE BOWDOIN METHOD

Lesson 6

Pop! Pop! Pop!

What You Need: A skillet, some margarine and popcorn for popping.

Why: To teach your child how to learn words and develop understandings while having fun with you.

What You Do: When you are grocery shopping, pick up a bag of unpopped corn. When you have time with your child, talk about what you two will be doing.

Remember . . . talk while you prepare. Let your child do as much as possible. For example, your child may be able to *open* the *bag* for you and to stand in a chair beside you as you put the popcorn in the *skillet* in the *margarine*. Cover the skillet with a *pot lid*. Talk about *what will happen when it gets hot!*

Talk about the sounds you hear as the popcorn pops. What does it say? Yes, *pop, pop, pop* (or *crack! crack!*).

Talk about *lifting the lid to peek.* Tell your child what you are doing when you *stir* to *keep it from burning. Sprinkle salt* (let your child do this). Put it in a *bowl* and let him eat! Talk about the size and color of the bowl.

What fun! What remembrances when your child grows up! Besides, he'll learn twenty or more word meanings!

Read the following. Encourage your child to clap with you as you read it . . . chant it so he can clap in time!

"Jump! Jump! Jump!
The popcorn dances round!
Pop! Pop! Pop!
It makes a popping sound!
I just can't wait
To take a little bite!
Yummy, yummy, yum!
It tastes just right!"

* * * * * * * * * * * * *

"Up and down, up and down.
Pops the popcorn all around!
It pops and pops 'til fluffy white.
Each piece in size a little bite!"

THE BOWDOIN METHOD

Lesson 7

Pots And Pans

What You Need: Pots and pans from the kitchen.

Why: To develop understandings and word meanings.

What You Do: Mother, do some of the following things. Remember to "talk in adult language"... it is best not to "talk down" to your child. This is the way he learns words—by *hearing them over and over* and by *doing* things which bring meaning to the words!

1. Take out two or three pots and/or pans. Let your child tell you the biggest... which will *hold* the *most*, which is the *smallest?*

2. Get out two pans that are *round* and one that is *square*. Show your child the *difference*. Pick up one pan, ask your child to find *another* one just *like it*. (Your child needs to understand these words when he enters school.)

3. Show your child the square pan. Show him the *sides* of the pan... and the *bottom* of the pan. Help him *count* the sides. Say, "There are four sides to this square pan. Count with me."

4. Get out two pots with lids. Get one smaller than the other. Mix the lids and see if your child can find the right lid for each pot. (This teaches your child to think! His brain is developing.)

5. Ask your child, "What are pots and pans used for?" (Encourage him to tell you... then praise him!) Talk about *cooking, vegetables, cake, macaroni, beans,* or any other ways your use your *utensils.*

Say this with your child:

"Peas porridge hot, peas porridge cold,
Peas porridge in the pot
Nine days old.
Some like it hot, some like it cold,
Some like it in the pot
Nine days old."

Did you ever play this? Perhaps an older child did!

COMPLIMENT YOUR CHILD
Mother, in this lesson your child may learn the meaning of 25 or more words... please do it!

THE BOWDOIN METHOD

Lesson 8

I'm A Little Teapot...

What You Need: A teapot or a kettle that you have in your kitchen.
Why: To teach word meanings and develop understandings.
What You Do: Show your child a teapot or a kettle.
Ask: "What is this *used* for?" (Yes, *boiling* water.)
"Is this water *hot* or *cold*?"
"How do you make it hot?" (Explain about *wood*, coal, *electricity* or gas.)
"Will it burn if it touches you?" (We must be careful!)

Ask about the *color* of the pot or the kettle (if it is made of metal, tell your child this).
Talk about the *spout* used for *pouring*.
Talk about the *handle* and what it is used for.
Tell your child that this is *useful*; mother *uses* it in the *kitchen*.
She may put it on the *stove*.
It must be used by *big boys* and *girls* or *older people*.

Your older children may have learned the song, "I'm a Little Teapot Short and Stout." If they know it, get them to sing and "act it out" with your little one.
Tell your child to look at the teapots at the *bottom* of this *page*.
Show him the *handle*.
Show him the *spout*.
Show him the *top*.
Ask which two are alike; how is one *different?*

Lesson 9

Spools And Pipe Cleaners

What You Need: Empty spools and pipe cleaners. (These are inexpensive, and your child can enjoy doing many things with them.)

Why: To teach your child new understanding which will help when he begins school.

What You Do: There are so many things your child can do with empty spools. *Save them.* Put them in a coffee can or box. You will be surprised what your child can do with them.

1. Let your child count spools. Show me two spools. Show me four spools. (Always compliment for correct response!) If you have some spools larger than the others, let your child show you the big ones (*large*), little ones (*small*), or in a *group of three find the one that is different.*

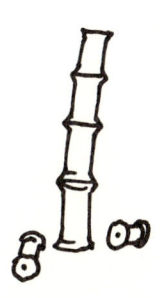

2. Let your child stack spools and make towers. *Tall one, small one.* See how high he can make it without falling.

3. If you can save as many as ten or more spools, let your little one take a shoestring and thread them all together. You may tie it around his neck for a necklace!

4. Make a lawn mower. Take a spool. Put one end of a pipe cleaner into the hole. Push it through until it comes out the other end. Twist the two ends of the pipe cleaner together and you have a lawn mower. Animals may be made from the pipe cleaners, also.

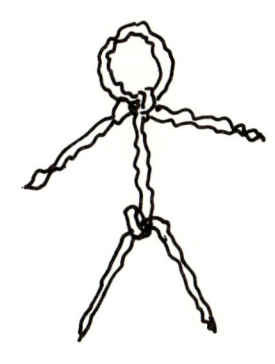

5. Use them to play dolls. The spools can be chairs. Put four together and cardboard on top for a table. Let your child cut food (use blunt scissors) for the table.

6. Show your child *how to make a person from a pipe cleaner*—round for head (twist). Make two arms by wrapping another pipe cleaner around. Help him make a whole family. Talk about who will be *tallest,* etc. Encourage much talk as your child plays.

THE BOWDOIN METHOD

PAGE 15

Lesson 10

Play Telephone

What You Need: A plastic bottle . . . empty bleach bottle or detergent bottle.

Why: To help you encourage your youngster to talk, to learn new word meanings and develop understandings.

What You Do: Cut out an opening in the bottle. Have your child hold the cut out opening of the bottle against his ear.

Encourage your child to speak into the bottle. His voice will be returned to his ear and he can hear, in a loud tone, his own speech! This will be fun for him!

Make believe — Since all children this age like "make believe," take two of the plastic bottles and pretend that they are telephones.

Talk about *dialing, answering* the phone, *"Who's calling?" "To whom do you wish to speak?"* Carry on a conversation. *"Talk quietly." "Speak loudly, grandmother has difficulty hearing."*

(Remember you are talking "adult" language. Your child will be gaining many new word meanings as you talk. Use different ways of saying things! Use BIG words . . . you will be surprised how quickly your child will learn them if you use them over and over.)

THIS IS PREPARATION FOR SCHOOL. THIS WILL HELP YOUR CHILD GET A HEAD START.

Ask your child to telephone someone that you name and give an *important message*. Tell your child what you wish him to say. See if he can remember the message. (This helps develop memory.)

Encourage your child to telephone his friend (make believe).

Read this poem:
Ting-a-ling!
Ding, ding!
I hear
The telephone ring.
"Hello, hello,
How are you?"
"Fine, fine
Thank you,
Thank you!"
"Yes! Yes!
I'll come to play."
"May I go Mom?
May I go today?"
"Yes! Yes!
She said I may."
"I'll be there
Right away!
. . . Goodbye!"

Read the poem several times.
See if your child can tell you what is happening.

THE BOWDOIN METHOD

Lesson 11

Telling Time

What You Need: A clock or watch.
Why: To teach understandings about time and numbers.

What You Do: Tell your child what a *clock* or a *watch* is used for . . . *time to get up, time to go to bed, time to eat.* Show your child the hands on the clock . . . the *long hand* and the *short hand*.

Talk about his own little *hands* and how they are *different* from hands on the clock. Ask: "What do you do with your hands?" (Encourage your child to talk . . . to think!) Ask which is *bigger*, the clock or the watch? Which is *smaller?*

Show your child the *numbers on the clock.* Tell him when he goes to school he will learn about them. *Count to twelve* with him . . . let him count after you. Show him the 12 at the *top;* the 6 at the *bottom*.

PRAISE YOUR CHILD FOR CORRECT RESPONSES!

Read the following poem . . . enjoy it yourself and he will "catch" your enthusiasm.

"Hickory, dickory, dock
The mouse ran up the clock!
The clock struck one!
The mouse ran down!
Hickory, dickory, dock
Tick-tock."

Ask your child what a clock says . . . "tick-tock; tick-tock."

See if your child is able to tell you why the mouse ran down.

Mother, please go over this lesson again and again until your little one understands the words and meanings you are teaching!

He will learn twenty or more word meanings from this lesson.

THE BOWDOIN METHOD

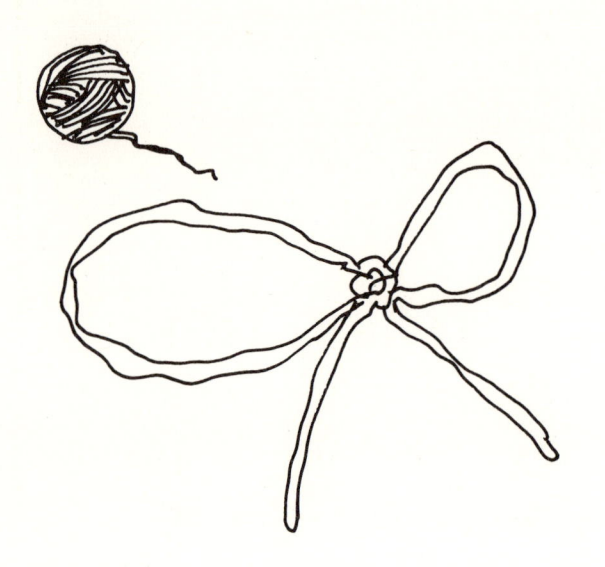

Lesson 12

Tying Is Fun

What You Need: A piece of string or yarn about a yard or more long.

Why: To teach your child some of the skills of thinking. To teach your child to listen and follow directions.

What You Do: Tell your child that this is a *string . . . yarn*. What do we do with a string? (Encourage your child to think—tie up packages, tie a balloon, tie my pigtails, tease my cat.)

Say: "I can do *something else*. I can tie your *hands together*!" (Tie your child's *wrists* together . . . he will smile! "Can you move your hands? Why not? Shall we untie them? I made a *bow knot* so that it would *untie*. Wasn't that fun?"

(Use lots of words—your child learns from your talk!)

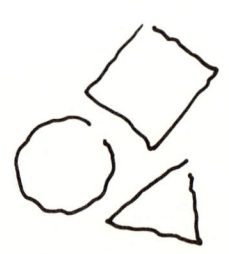

Make shapes with your string.
Make a *circle* with the string. Ask your child *what shape* this is. If he doesn't know "circle," tell him . . . a circle is *round*.

Now, take up the string and let him try to make a circle. (Help him if he needs help.) Compliment!

Make a *square* with the string. Ask your child what shape this is. If he doesn't know, tell him a square is like a *box*. It has *four sides* . . . one, two, three, four. Let your child count with you.

Now, take up the string and let your child try to make a square. This is hard to do . . . but if you *cut the string* into four *pieces* your child can do it.

Make a *triangle* with a string or with three pieces of string. Ask your child what this shape is. Count the sides. Then let your child make a triangle and count the sides with you.

Play a game. Make the string into a circle. Tell your child you are going to give some *directions* . . . some *instructions*. (Your child needs to know these when he goes to school.)

Step *over* your circle.
Stand *in* your circle.
Step *out of* your circle.
Walk *around* your circle.

These are words your child will need to know in school.
Don't forget . . . COMPLIMENT!

PAGE 18

THE BOWDOIN METHOD

Lesson 13

What's In The Sack?

What You Need: A paper sack and any items which you may find around the house, such as a spoon, saucer, cup, sock, pencil, spool, etc.

Why: To develop your child's ability to touch and think about what he feels and to identify it.

What You Do: Play the game, *What is it?* Have your child close his eyes while you place an object in a paper sack. Then, let him feel in the sack (without looking) and see if he can tell you by the "feel" what the object is.

REMEMBER... COMPLIMENT WHEN YOUR CHILD GUESSES CORRECTLY!

Make the game fun! Help your child feel that learning can be fun.

I Have a Secret in a Sack

After you have played the game using several objects, change the game and play *I Have a Secret in the Sack*. When your child has his eyes closed, place something in the sack. Describe what you have in the sack, and let your child guess from your description. (This teaches your child word meaning... as well as listening and thinking!)

For example:
I have a secret in the sack.
It is something we use at the table.
We use it when we eat our soup.
We use it when we eat our cereal.
We wash it after a meal.
What is my secret?

or

I have a secret in the sack.
It is something to wear.
Girls wear it on their hair.
Boys do not wear it.
What is my secret?
(COMPLIMENT... FOR CORRECT ANSWERS)

Mother, there are many possibilities here. You are teaching your child many word meanings. And he is having fun!

Make your lessons short... your child cannot sit still very long.

THE BOWDOIN METHOD

PAGE 19

Lesson 14

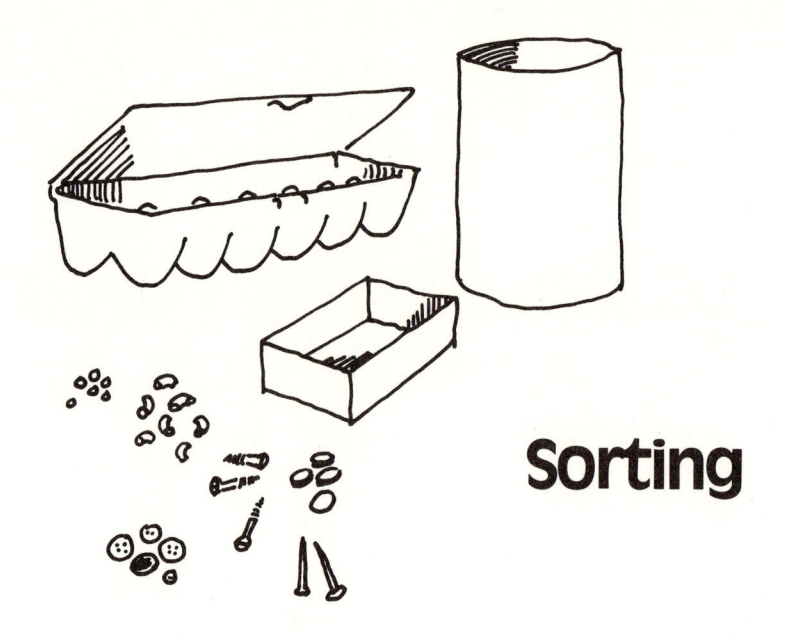

Sorting

What You Need: Empty egg carton; a container, such as a coffee can or box to put an assortment of things in; and an assortment of things like buttons, screws, dried beans, peas, corn, pennies, bits of macaroni or any other small thing which may be found around the house.

Why: To teach your child to sort things that are alike, to be able to see them and pick them out. (This is a skill which will help him learn to read more easily.)

What You Do: Give your child either an egg carton or muffin pans.

Let him sit on the floor. Explain that you want him to pick out all the corn and put them in this section, all the buttons here, all the macaroni here. (Put one thing in each section.)

Encourage your child to *find* everything that is *alike* and put it *together* in one of the places.

If you find that little things are too small for your child to *sort,* then get larger things, such as spools, color crayons, pencils, blocks and let him put them in small pans. Call this game *Sorting Fun*.

If your child is not able to find the things that are alike, show him and let him try again!

WHY IS THIS IMPORTANT?

Your child needs training in seeing things, sorting things, picking out things, handling things.

This has to be developed before he is able to see letters in a word. (This is readiness for reading.)

ALWAYS MAKE YOUR LESSON WITH YOUR LITTLE ONE FUN! AND NEVER LEAVE HIM ALONE WITH THE MATERIALS!

Make it *short* . . . don't let him tire or get bored!

Always talk . . . talk . . . talk . . . while you play. Your child will be learning what words mean! He needs to know *many word meanings*.

You may encourage an older son or daughter to do this lesson or other lessons with your child. Let your older child know that you appreciate this help . . . and this will help his feelings too!

GRANDMOTHERS! They are wonderful with your child, they seem to have so much patience!

THE BOWDOIN METHOD

Lesson 15

Things Around The House

What You Need: Household items, such as cup and saucer; fork and spoon; shoe and sock; penny and nickle; brush and comb; glass and milk carton; paper and pencil . . . and any other things which you think will help you.

Why: To help your child *learn to think;* to think about things that belong together or that *go together.* (This helps develop your child's brain.)

What You Do: After you have found some items in the house which belong *together,* place three of them in front of your child on a table or on the floor.

Let your child tell you the name of the items . . . for example, penny, shoe, sock.

Ask: *Which two belong together?* Yes, the shoe and sock go together because we wear them on our feet! (If your child cannot tell you, you tell him and let him try again.)

Then take three other items, such as shoe, saucer, cup. See if your child can name the items and can tell you that the saucer and cup *belong together.*

Change to the brush, comb, paper and keep repeating until your child understands *relationships.*

(He will be asked to do this when he begins school in his first readiness book. He will be using pictures. He will be ready for this activity if you have helped at home with the real objects.)

Suggestions for things that go together: Cup-saucer, glove-mitten, shoe-sock, pencil-paper, knife-fork, big book-little book. (You can think of many others.)

After your child has learned to select the things that go together, you may play other games with the objects, such as:

1. I am thinking of something that I use for *writing. What is it?* (Compliment your child if he can tell you.)

2. *Which is missing?* Put down about four objects. Let child close his eyes while you remove one of the objects. He opens his eyes and guesses which one you took away.

3. Play *Hide the Object.* Let your child close his eyes while you hide it in the room. Then let your child open his eyes and find the object while you describe where you have put it. For example: "It is under something that is way up high . . . it is in a corner far away from you." (As you talk, your child will be learning word meanings! Remember, he needs so many . . . THOUSANDS!)

THE BOWDOIN METHOD

PAGE 21

Lesson 16

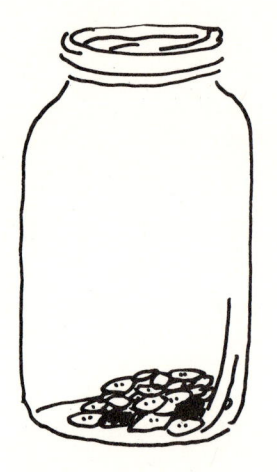

Buttons Are Fun

What You Need: Buttons which you may cut off old clothing which is no longer used. (Keep these in a jar. They are very useful for teaching many things to young children.)

Why: To teach likeness and difference, sorting according to size and color, and visual memory.

What You Do:

1. Place three buttons before your child, *two that are alike* and one that is *different*. Tell your child to *show you the two that are alike*. (If he cannot do this, show him.) Ask your child to show you the *button that is different* . . . not like the others.

2. Give your child several buttons of different sizes. See if he can find for you the *biggest button*, the *smallest one*.

3. Give your child several buttons. Pick up one. Ask your child to find one just like yours.

4. If you have buttons that are assorted colors, let your child find all the white buttons and put them together, the red ones, black ones. This is sorting.

5. See if your child can *copy a design* which you make with buttons. (This helps in visual training.) For example, you make a line of little buttons and put a big one on the end or in the middle. Tell your child to make one just like yours! (He must be able to do this before he is ready to look at the letters in a word!)

6. If you have buttons of different sizes, let your child pick out all the large ones and put them together, all the small ones. (This is also sorting . . . but according to size.)

7. Let your child put the buttons in a jar while you count with him (only to five in the beginning).

8. Encourage your child to practice buttoning and unbuttoning his clothing.

REMEMBER . . . COMPLIMENT YOUR CHILD FOR TRYING!

PAGE 22

THE BOWDOIN METHOD

Lesson 17

Paper Dolls

What You Need: Newspaper and scissors.

Why: To help develop awareness of body parts and number concepts.

What You Do: Tell your child that you are going to cut something while he watches.

Take your newspaper and fold so that you can cut several dolls at once. (Remember to cut one arm on the fold in order that the dolls will hold hands.)

Talk about *folding* the paper. "Now I will *cut* it *this* way, and I'll turn the corner and make *something round*. *Guess* what I am *making*." (Encourage your child to guess . . . he is learning the meaning of the word "guess" which he will need to know in school.) Keep talking as you cut.

Then, open up the paper dolls and "laugh" with your child about the surprise! Your child will probably say, "Do it again." This time make *bigger* dolls or *smaller* dolls. Fold the paper so that sometimes you will make *more* dolls and sometimes *fewer*.

Count the dolls with your child (go from left to right). Talk about the dolls holding hands.

Ask: "Do they all look *alike* or *different*?" Help your child to see that they are all just alike.

Read this poem to your child:
"Cut, cut
A head,
Cut, cut
Some feet!
Cut, cut
Some arms,
Cut, cut
How neat!"

"Cut, cut,
Snap, snap,
Paper dolls
Dress and cap!"

"The scissors go
Zooming away!
Paper dolls
Now I can play!"

"My Mommy cuts
One, two, three
Paper dolls
For baby and me!"

"I like my dolls
And paper too,
Would you like some?
Would you, would you?"

THE BOWDOIN METHOD

PAGE 23

Lesson 18

Hands Are Helpers

What You Need: A piece of paper and a color crayon.

Why: To develop understanding and appreciation for self.

What You Do: Talk to your child about how many things he can do with his hands.

Let him think of as many as he can. You help by suggesting some.

Outline the shape of your child's hand on a piece of paper. Talk to your child all the time you are doing this, "Here we go, around the *little finger*, around the *ring finger*, around the *big finger*, around the *pointer* and now the *thumb* all the way to your *wrist*."

When you have finished, *count the fingers* with your child. Then, outline the shape of your hand as you talk.

Tell your child to look at *both* hands. Which is your *hand?* Which is my *hand?* How do the hands look *alike?* How are they *different?* Which hand is *biggest?* Which is the *smallest?* Draw *fingernails* and *knuckles* on the hands. Show him what you are doing. (When you finish, let him color the hands.)

Ask your child:
 Could you write without your hands?
 Could you draw without your hands?
 Could you put on your clothes without your hands?
 Could you eat without your hands?
 My! What good helpers our hands are!
 (Help your child think!)

Talk about washing hands before eating, keeping hands clean, using our hands for nice things for helping others—not for fighting and hitting!

End: "What nice hands you have! I like them!" (Build good feelings!)

PAGE 24

THE BOWDOIN METHOD

Lesson 19

Shadow Play

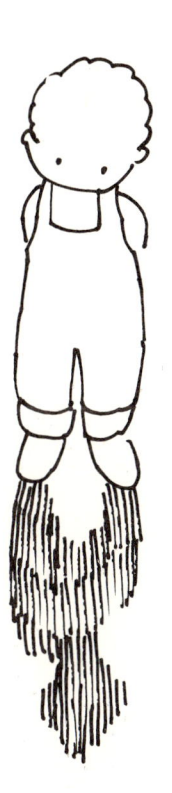

What You Need: Nothing.

Why: To help your child gain new understandings, to know the meanings of many words (20,000 to 48,000 before he starts to school!).

What You Do: Take your child outside on a sunny day and show him his shadow.

Show him how it moves when he moves.

Sometimes his shadow is *long*; sometimes his shadow is *short*. Let him see his shadow at *different times* of the day in order that he can see how it changes.

If there isn't a sunny day, your child can see his shadow by the light in the room at night.

Let him see your shadow, too, and point out that it is *bigger* than his shadow.

Let him have fun outside. "See if he can 'catch' his shadow!"

Show your child how to make "shadow animals" by putting the hands together, some fingers up for the ears; wiggle the fingers and make the ears wiggle! Do this between the light and the wall. This can be much fun for your child . . . and older children may like to play this with your little one!

Read this poem to your child:
"I have a friendly shadow
That belongs to only me.
If you will look where I am
My shadow you will see.
It runs and jumps and dances
And sways to and fro.
It's with me when I reach for the sky
Or bend to touch my toe."

THE BOWDOIN METHOD

PAGE 25

Lesson 20

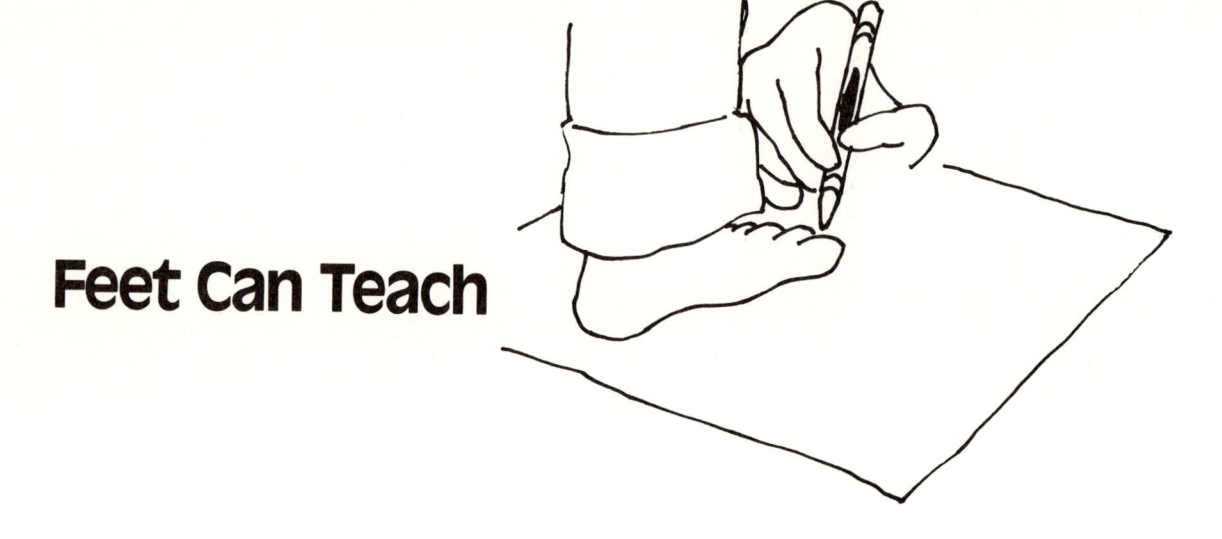

Feet Can Teach

What You Need: Your child's feet, a color crayon and a sheet of paper.

Why: To teach your child many understandings and word meanings.

What You Do: Have your child *take off* his shoes. Let him stand on a piece of paper while you *draw around* his foot. (Talk to him all the time you are doing this . . . tell him what you are doing. This is the way he learns what words mean. Something like: "*Stand firmly* on the *page* . . . *really still* while I *draw around your foot.* Here I go around the *sides* of your foot, around the *heel*, now here is the *little toe*, now I'll go *between* your toes! Does that tickle?")

"My, just look at your foot!" (Build enthusiasm . . . be excited as if this is something great!)

The talk about *one foot, two feet.*

1. What do we do with our feet? Yes, they are *very useful* to us . . . they help us walk. Could we walk without them? How do some people walk who do not have feet? What *else* do we do? *(Skip, run, jump, hop.)*

2. What do we wear on our feet? Why do we wear shoes? (Encourage your child to THINK! This develops his brain.)

3. *How many toes* do you have? Let's count them. (Mother, count with your child . . . let him count after you.) Yes, we have five toes. Which is your *little toe?* Your *big toe?* (Encourage your child to say the complete sentence after you. WHEN HE DOES THIS, PRAISE HIM!)

4. Let your child do these actions as you say them with him: Feet *walk;* feet *skip;* feet *hop;* feet *run.* PRAISE HIM FOR LEARNING!

5. Take your child in your lap. Say this nursery rhyme while pulling his toes:

"This little pig went to market.
This little pig stayed at home.
This little pig had roast beef.
This little pig had none.
This little pig said, 'Wee, wee, wee,'
All the way home!"

(He may say, "Do it again!"; if he doesn't, repeat it anyway. Tell him this is just *pretend . . . make believe.* My, what fun for your little one!)

Lesson 21

Learning About The Body

What You Need: Black crayon and piece of paper.

Why: To teach your child to appreciate himself and to make him aware of the parts of his body and their use.

What You Do:

1. The *Sesame Street* program suggests this chant to help your child learn his body parts. What fun for your child! (Let your child point as you chant.)

"Shoulders, shoulders
I have shoulders,
(child's name) has shoulders, too!
"Elbows, elbows
I have elbows,
(child's name) has elbows, too!
"Nose, nose
I have a nose,
(child's name) has a nose, too!
"Ears, ears
I have ears,
(child's name) has ears, too"

Do the same for parts of the body, especially those your child does not know — knees, ankles, hips, chest, thumb, fingers, neck, stomach.

2. Play "I Am Thinking"

I am thinking of something you use for walking. What is it?

I am thinking of something you use for hearing. What is it?

I am thinking of something you use for clapping. What is it?

I am thinking of something you use for seeing. What are they?

3. *Touch*

Touch parts of your child's body. Let him tell you what you are touching. COMPLIMENT WHEN HE GETS IT CORRECT!

4. Give your child a large black crayon and tell your child to make himself. If he makes the arms coming out from the head, this is natural at this age. You may encourage, but *don't do it for him*. This would make him feel he can't *do*. You may give simple directions such as: "Did you make the hair?" or "What about the legs?"

Remember: You are encouraging your child to think . . . *not* teaching him to draw.

THE BOWDOIN METHOD

Lesson 22

Washday Fun

What You Need: Clothes that you wash and hang on the line.
Why: To teach your child the names of clothing and other understandings about sizes, colors.

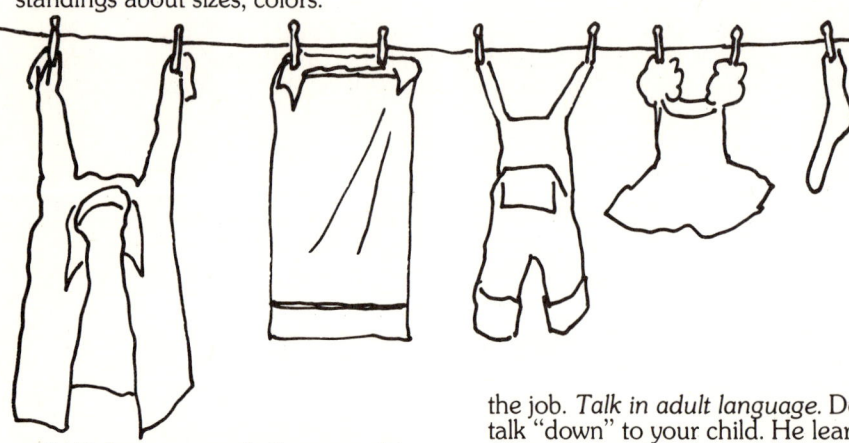

1. *Talk as you work.* Say something like: "Here is Mother's purple blouse. I'll hang it up first. Would you like to hand me the clothespins as I need them? I'll need two clothespins."

As you take out each piece, tell your child the *name* of the garment, the *color,* and *who wears it.* (There is much learning here!)

Talk about the *big pieces* such as sheets, the *little pieces.* Talk about shapes such as the *square pieces* (diapers), the *round* doilies.

2. When you have finished hanging out the clothes, let your little one *see* if he can find his own clothes. Talk about having finished *(completed)* the job. *Talk in adult language.* Don't talk "down" to your child. He learns the meaning of many words when you talk to him as you would talk to a friend, although you may need to say it several different ways, such as: "Now, we have *finished* our work. We have completed our job. Now, we are through!"

3. If there is time, count the shirts, the dresses, the skirts, or the sheets. *Count with your child.*

4. When the clothes are taken in and you fold them, let him fold the little things such as the wash cloths.

Talk about *folding, separating* the colored clothes for *ironing, sprinkling, putting away.* THANK YOUR CHILD FOR HELPING.

(Your child will be happy and feel secure and a part of the family group if he feels that he is helping you!)

5. Give your child several socks that you have washed and let him find the mates. Say, "Find another sock just like this one and put them together." (This is the first step in reading readiness . . . finding things *alike, different.*) Your child may sort by colors, by size, by design.

PAGE 28

THE BOWDOIN METHOD

Ironing And Learning

What You Need: An iron and clothing to iron.

Why: To teach your child new word meanings and understanding as you work.

What You Do: Sometimes as you are ironing, talk to your little one.

Say something similar to the following:

"I am working. I am ironing. The iron is hot. Steam is coming out. Hear the *steam go ssizz!*"

"I go *around* and around, I *press hard.* I get out the *wrinkles.*"

"I am ironing a *dress.* What *color* is the dress? Yes! It is blue. It is a blue dress." (Talk in complete sentences—this is how your child learns words . . . as he hears them!)

"Now, I put the dress on a *hanger*" . . . or "now, I *fold* the *shirt* like this . . . one, two, three, four, five, six little buttons."

"And when I fold it, I put it on the bed. When I am finished, I will put it away in the drawer for you to wear."

(Your child learns many new words from hearing you and watching you! Please give him this opportunity!)

Pretend:

Let your child pretend to iron as you iron. Give your child a scrap . . . or a little piece of your ironing. Give a plastic cup or something to pretend it is an iron. He or she will have fun folding and ironing little pieces . . . bath cloths, handkerchiefs.

Ask: Which is *hot?* Which is *cold?*

Read this to your child over and over:

Iron! Iron!
Iron the clothes.
Clean shirts.
Clean pants.
Clean dress.
Clean hose!

Mother works,
works all day.
Washes, irons!
And I run and play!

I love to iron
My doll clothes, too.
Let me, Mamma,
Please do!

Lesson 24

Shoes Can Teach

What You Need: Two pairs of shoes; one pair larger than the other.

Why: To teach word meanings, likenesses and differences, size and color.

What You Do: Place the shoes on the floor. Talk about a *pair* of shoes; *two pairs* of shoes.

1. Ask your child to find you the bigger pair of shoes; the *smaller* pair. Always compliment when he does this. If he doesn't know, tell him. Then ask again.

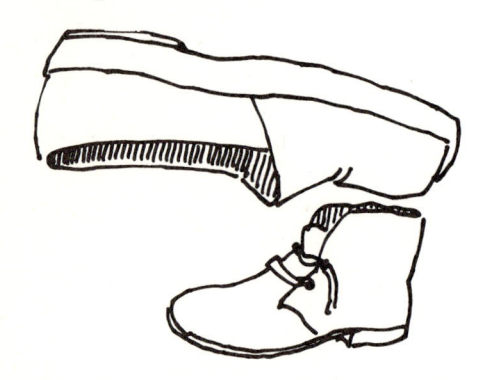

2. Mix up the shoes. Take one shoe and ask your child to find another that *matches* it . . . that is *just like* the one you are *holding* up. (Try to help him find it. This is important to reading readiness. Children need to see things that are alike and things that are different.)

3. Ask your child to find a shoe that is *different from* the one you hold. (Help him understand what "different" means . . . this takes much repetition with other objects.)

4. Ask your child to find the smaller pair of shoes.

5. To help him learn to think, ask your child to find the pair of shoes that would be the *size* for mother, sister, daddy, or baby. See if he can *relate size of shoes to size of person*. ALWAYS COMPLIMENT!

6. Talk to your child about *different kinds of shoes,* boots, sandals, houseshoes, overshoes, tennis shoes. And talk about the *colors of the shoes* which you have.

7. Encourage your child to tell you *why we wear shoes*. Enjoy this poem. Read it over several times.

"I have rings on my fingers.
I have shoes on my feet.
When the snowman comes to visit
Shoes are very hard to beat!
"Shoes may be big or little
They may be rough or neat.
It doesn't really matter
Just so they fit my feet!"

8. Begin teaching your child how to tie his shoelaces. This takes much practice but it will be important when he begins school. He will be pleased with himself!

THE BOWDOIN METHOD

Lesson 25

Chasing Fireflies

What You Need: A small jar with holes punched in the lid.

Why: To use things in nature to help your child develop word meanings.

What You Do: When summer comes, there may be many fireflies in your yard.

Just before it gets too dark, encourage your child to catch some fireflies and put them in a jar.

Tell your child the following things about a firefly:

 1. Another name for him is "lightning bug".

 2. Something in his body helps him make the light... two chemicals which mix with oxygen (air) he breathes in and helps to burn to make the light.

 3. Scientists are not really sure why the lightning bug lights up. They think it is how they find their mates.

Let your child count the number of fireflies he catches.

Always encourage him to let them fly away when he is through so that other people can enjoy watching them flash their little lights on and off in the night sky.

As your child lets them fly away, one at a time, encourage him to tell you how many are left.

Read this poem, and talk about it with your child. If you enjoy poetry, your child will catch your enthusiasm and enjoy it also! Encourage him to listen to the rhythm and listen for the rhyming words.

 Fireflies
 "Firefly, Firefly
 Light your tail!
 High up you fly
 With your sail
 All lighted up
 For us to see—
 Mom, Dad,
 Granny and me!"

THE BOWDOIN METHOD

Lesson 26

Leaves Teach

What You Need: Several leaves from the yard. If you do not have trees, use the pictures on this page.

Why: To teach likenesses and differences, shapes and colors, and sizes. There are many concepts you can teach your little one with this simple lesson on leaves.

What You Do: If it is possible, *gather leaves* with your child. See how many *different kinds* and *shapes* you can *find*. See how many words you may talk about as you do this together. (This is the way your child learns . . . by first-hand experience.)

Some of the things you may do with your child:

1. Talk to him about leaves. Tell him they grow on the trees, and when *Fall* comes they fall off and new little *baby leaves* will grow again *next Spring* and pop open in a *bud* and *grow* into a *big leaf.* (Your child will enjoy your telling him this.) Talk about how the

limb looks without the leaves . . . and in Winter show him the bumps on the limbs which hold the baby leaves.

2. Talk about the *beautiful colors* in the fall leaves—brown, orange, yellow, green. See if he can match colors.

"Find me *another* green leaf like this."

"Find me a yellow leaf like this."
PRAISE FOR CORRECT RESPONSE!

3. Take three leaves, *two alike* and one *different*. Ask your child to show you two that are alike (in shape). Fine the one that is *different*. (Remember, your child will not understand these word meanings until you have used them again and again!)

4. Ask questions that require your child to THINK. (You are helping his brain develop!)

"Which leaf is the *largest (biggest)?*" (Show just 3 leaves.)
"Which leaf is *smallest (least)?*

5. Trace around some leaves. Let your child color one brown, one green, one yellow. DON'T MAKE HIM STAY WITHIN THE LINES. His muscles are not developed yet!

THE BOWDOIN METHOD

Lesson 27

Backyard World

What You Need: Nothing.

Why: To teach your child many new words and understandings.

What You Do: *This is a nature lesson.*

Nature can be very meaningful to your little one, but it takes a little time! Talk whenever the occasion arises:

a bunny running *across the yard,*
a squirrel scurrying up a tree,
a robin on the lawn in the Spring,
starlings eating in the yard,
a butterfly flitting about,
fireflies in the summer (What fun to catch!).

Teach your child to have "sharp eyes"—to observe, to see, to talk! This is HOW YOUR CHILD LEARNS! Encourage your child to look out the window and see how many birds he can see. Talk to your child about birds. Tell him some of the following facts:

About the mother bird and the father bird working together to build their nest. Talk about the mother laying three or four little eggs, sitting on them and about the babies hatching. Father bird watches and brings food to the mother while she sits. The father bird is the brightest and prettiest color; mother is dull so she can't be seen easily. Tell about the mother and father feeding the babies bugs and worms, until they get large enough to fly. Tell how the birds use string, feathers, grass, and sticks to build their nest.

(Your little one will love to hear you talk about real things.)

Encourage your child to watch for birds.

Talk about the color of the bird and, if you know, always tell the name of the bird.

Help your child to be friendly with birds because they are our helpers. They eat bugs that destroy crops and gardens.

If you have scraps, sunflower seeds, or fat suet, let your child feed the birds in the winter. Put the food out, and birds will come to it—a lesson right at your own back door!

How can you help your child understand 20,000 to 40,000 words and to know how to use them; 3,000 to 6,000 when he starts to school? (He needs this to be really successful!) By TALKING, READING, TELLING, ASKING, SHOWING THINGS, TAKING LITTLE TRIPS! Use things of nature to help you.

THE BOWDOIN METHOD — PAGE 33

Lesson 28

Neighborhood Classroom

What You Need: Nothing.

Why: To teach your child many new words and understandings.

To teach your child to observe things, to be able to talk about what he sees, and to learn word meanings.

What You Do: Take your child for a walk up or down the street and in the neighborhood.

As you walk along, let your child tell you what he sees:

big trees—little trees,
big shrubs—little shrubs,
big houses—little houses,
curtains at the windows,
green grass,
an ant hill,
dandelions,
flowers peeping out of the ground,
stoplight,
curb at the end of the block,
a fire hydrant,
cars passing by—trucks, what kinds of trucks,
people—little and big.

Talk about the *colors* of the things your child sees. See how many *different* colors of cars your child can see.

Talk about the *sizes* of the things.

When you return home (after a few minutes... but with much talk), give your child a large crayon and some paper (newspaper will do) and tell him to make something he saw on his walk. If your child says, "I can't," say: "Oh, yes you can! Come, I'll get your crayons and help you get started!" (He needs confidence.)

When the picture is finished, a wise parent will *not* ask, "What did you make?" (Your child thinks anybody should know!) Say: *"Tell me about your picture."*

Compliment!

Put the picture up in the house so the family may see.

PAGE 34   THE BOWDOIN METHOD

Lesson 29

Watching Squirrels

What You Need: Use the picture of the squirrel on this page or, better still, if you live in a neighborhood in which there are trees and squirrels, observe one with your child.

Why: To teach word meanings . . . and to help your child enjoy poetry and rhyming words.

What You Do: Talk to your child about squirrels. Tell your child how the squirrel gets his *food* and about how he *hides nuts* and *acorns* under the *ground* and in a *hole* for his *winter food.* (Your child will love to hear.)

Talk about the big, *furry tail* and about how *fast* he can *scamper* up a *tree.* Talk about his ears, his feet, his eyes. Tell your child about the squirrel *building* a *nest high* up in a *tree.* If you can find one in your neighborhood, show it to your child. (Teach your child to watch for things of nature in your yard . . . this is learning that will help him in school.)

Talk about the color of the squirrel, the color of the nuts. Let your child point out the parts of the *squirrel's body* as you call them out to him. Ask your child if *he thinks* the *squirrel is smart?* Why?

"Squealy the squirrel
Climbs up the tree;
He sits at the top and looks at me.
"Squealy the squirrel
Runs down the tree;
He scampers away, Oh, where can he be!"

THE BOWDOIN METHOD

PAGE 35

Lesson 30

Learning With Rocks

What You Need: Rocks and a paper sack.

Why: To teach your child understandings and word meanings and to help him learn to observe things in nature.

What You Do: Take a walk with your child. Walk around the yard or in the neighborhood or in the countryside.

Help your child find rocks small enough that can be put in a paper bag.

Talk to him about the *size* of the rocks. Which is *smaller? larger?* Which rocks are *round?*

Let him put all the larger rocks in one pile. Put smaller rocks in another pile.

Select three rocks. Let your child tell you the *biggest, next to the biggest,* and the *smallest.* (He needs to understand these relationships.)

Tell your child: The rocks are *hard*—not *soft.*

Cotton is soft—cloth is soft.
Rocks are hard.
Some rocks are *little.*
Some rocks are *big.*
Some rocks are *rough.*
Some rocks are *smooth.* (Let him feel.)

Explain to your child that rocks are smooth because water has made them that way by washing them. Tell him that rocks hold soil together. This keeps water from washing it away. Sometimes we may find a soft rock. It will *crumble.* But most rocks are hard.

Read this to your child. (Let your child clap as you chant! He'll like that!)

Big rocks—one, two
Little rocks—one, two
Soft rocks—one, two
Hard rocks—one, two
Rocks, rocks,
I like rocks!

This may lead your child to want to start a *rock collection.* Encourage this, and as you go about, look for unusual ones.

PAGE 36

THE BOWDOIN METHOD

Lesson 31

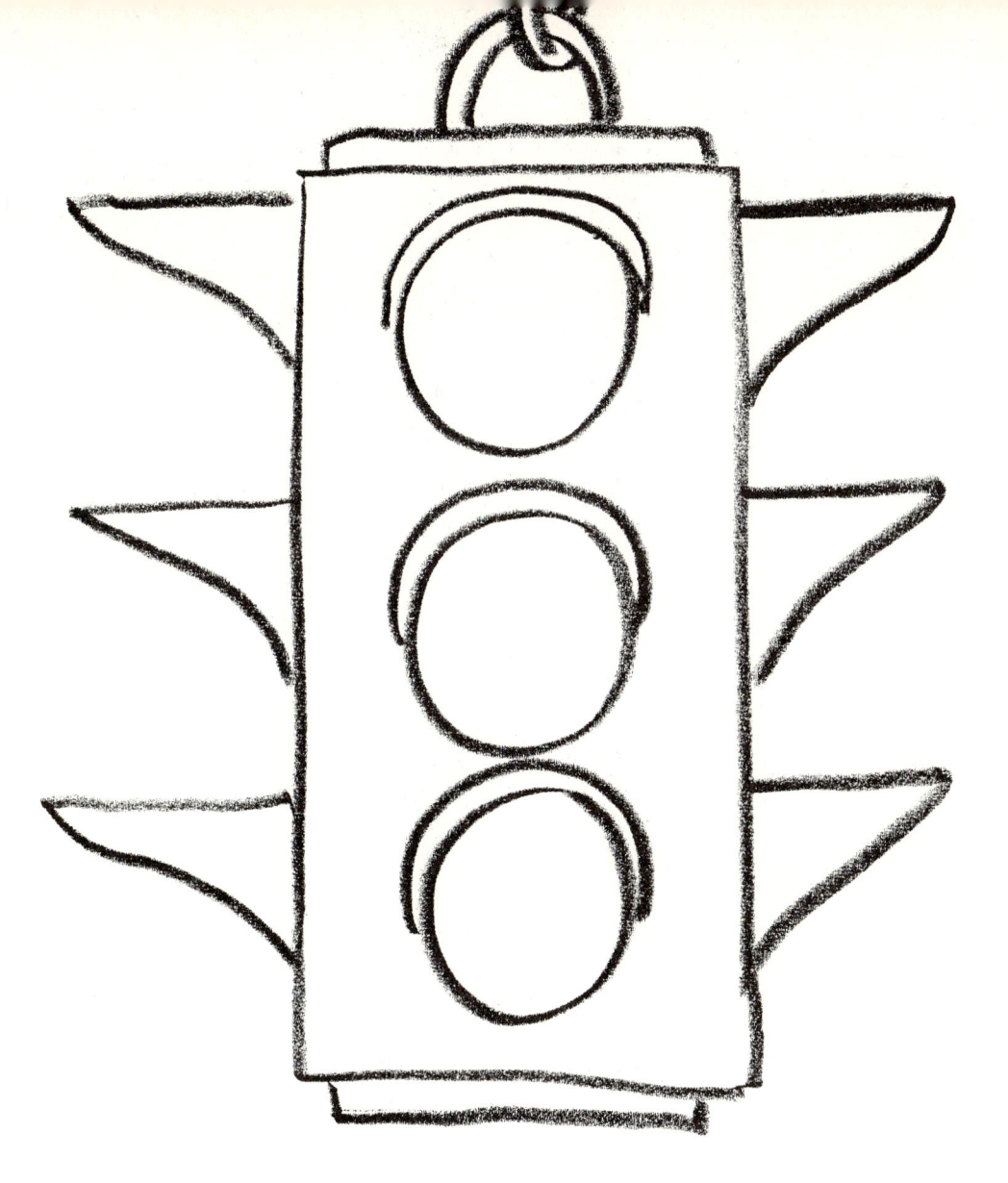

Red And Green, Stop And Go

What You Need: Crayons and paper.

Why: To develop a knowledge of safety on streets.

What You Do: Show your child a traffic light as you walk along the street or as you ride in a car.

Talk about the color of the lights. Tell your child *what the colors mean.* (Green means *go*; red means *stop*; yellow means *wait.*)

As the lights change, let your child tell you what the colors mean. Talk about the *lights changing.*

Explain why we have traffic lights. Talk about avoiding *accidents* and how the traffic lights help us to live *safely.* (Tell your child in several different ways in order that he may understand. Use adult language. Your child needs to hear words and to associate meanings.)

THIS IS HOW YOUR CHILD LEARNS.

Give your child his box of colors. Let him select the color that says go.
Let him select the color that says stop.
Let him select the color that says wait.

(Remember . . . compliment for correct answers!)

Ask your child to make some traffic signals . . . traffic lights. You may let him color the light in this book. Talk about the *shape* of the light. See if your child can tell you what "round" means.

THE BOWDOIN METHOD

PAGE 37

Lesson 32

Signs Talk

What You Need: Nothing.
Why: To observe signs and what they say, to learn differences in shapes and colors, and to talk in complete sentences.

What You Do: As you take a walk to the grocery or down the street and as you ride in a car, help your child look for signs—ALL KINDS AND COLORS AND SHAPES.

Point out the sign to your child. Tell him what *color* it is and *what shape* it is.

Some are *round;* some are *square;* some are *curved;* and some have *diamond* shape. Help your child notice the *different* shapes.

Tell your child that these signs tell us something . . . they have words on them. Tell him what the words say.

Let him repeat after you and encourage a complete statement: "The sign is red. It says STOP!"

Explain to your child why we have signs . . . just as rules at home or at school . . . to help us obey and be good citizens!

Sometimes play a game: See how many *different signs* we can see as we walk along. Count them. Or how many signs are green or red. Where are the street signs? The stop signs?

Say with your child: Signs, signs
All around.
Signs, signs
All over town!

Mother: This lesson may be done all during the year.

Your child learns through repeating!

This is the beginning of learning to read. You are not teaching your child to read, but you are certainly preparing him for reading. Reading is the most difficult skill which your child will ever learn.

All these things will help prepare him for his first year in school.

Besides . . . he will be talking and listening to you . . . the one he loves! How important this is!

THE BOWDOIN METHOD

Lesson 33

Listening, Not Looking

What You Need: A handkerchief for blindfolding.

Why: To teach your child to listen. To develop understandings. (This is important to his ability to learn.)

What You Do:

1. *Play a listening game.* Blindfold your child with the handkerchief. Say:
"Put on your
bunny ear
see what
you can hear."

Then make a noise for your child to guess. You may do such things as drop something on the floor, move a chair, tear paper, snap your finger, cough, clap your hands, scratch your head, and (if you are in the kitchen) turn on the water.

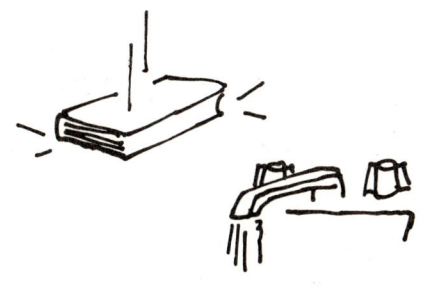

(Compliment your child when he guesses correctly the sound you make.)

2. *Pretend to be an animal.* See if your child can guess what animal you are when you:
cluck . . . cluck,
baa . . . baa,
moo . . . moo,
bow-wow . . . bow-wow,
quack . . . quack,
cock-a-doodle-do,
gobble . . . gobble,
peep . . . peep.

3. *See if your child can make sounds.* Tell him to show you:
How the car sounds.
How the fire engine sounds.
How the unhappy little baby cries.
How the clown laughs.
How mother sings the baby to sleep.
How the angry bear growls.

THE BOWDOIN METHOD

Lesson 34

Scary Faces

What You Need: Paper sack and color crayons.

Why: To teach new word meanings, to develop understandings of body parts, to have fun with your child at Halloween.

What You Do: Take a brown paper bag from the grocery. Pull the paper sack over your child's head (use lots of words — *sack, bag, brown, grocery, pull over, head,* etc.)

"*Now* . . . can you *see?* Why, of *course not*, because your *eyes* are covered. Show me where your *eyes* are." (Let him show you, then mark or tear the sack where the eyes should be.)

"Now where is your nose?" (Have him point.) "Now touch your mouth."

"*Up we go!* Let's *take it off* and make a mask. We will need our mask to have a face."

"What *kind* of face do we want? Shall we make a *scary face* for Halloween? Or a pretty face? Or a sad face, a happy face?"

When you have done this, cut or tear out the *eyes, nose, mouth* . . . talking all the time you are doing this.

Give him the big color crayons and help your child decide about what kind of face (mask) he will make.

Let him scribble! Don't expect a finished product.

If he wants a *funny face* . . . encourage him to make a big red mouth and a funny round nose like a *clown!*

After it is finished, let him put it on and look at himself in the *mirror*. Laugh with him. He will love this!

There are many things that you can do now, such as:

"Now you scare me! Say, 'Boo!'"

or

"*This is a happy face.* What would a happy person do?" (Sing, maybe . . . why not sing?)

or

If it is a sad face, what would a sad person do? (Would he cry?)

THE BOWDOIN METHOD

Lesson 35

Fun At Halloween

What You Need: A pumpkin and knife.

Why: To develop understandings from this experience with you. (Doing things with your child will make your child happy and secure and let him know that you love him!)

What You Do: While you work always do a lot of talking, this is how your child learns. Something like the following:

"Would you like to make a jack-o-lantern? Do you know what a *jack-o-lantern* is?" (Tell him.)

"Let's start with the *pumpkin* and a *sharp knife*. We must be *very* careful with the knife, so Mamma will use it with *care*."

"*First,* I'll *cut out* the *top*. Which is the top? The bottom? *Around* and around I go. *See,* what is inside? Look at the *seeds*. Let's *rake them out* in this pan (or on the paper)."

(Let your child help you with this. YES, OF COURSE IT'S MESSY! Show your child the seeds. Tell him about the little seeds being *planted* in the *ground, growing* a *vine* and making pumpkins.)

"Let's *put* a few out to *dry,* and we may *plant* them *when* Spring comes when the *weather* gets *warm,* and we may grow a pumpkin right in our *own yard!*"

"Now, what does our pumpkin need to make it a jack-o-lantern? Yes, some *eyes* . . . how many? A *nose?* And a *big mouth.*" (Cut and talk to your child while you do this.) "Shall we make a big *happy mouth?* Would you like to have him *smiling?* Shall we cut in some *teeth?*" (After you have finished, help him admire it!)

The older children would enjoy doing this lesson for you.

Mother: If you do not have a pumpkin which you can get easily, make one on paper. You may help your little one with *triangle* eyes, nose, and a smiling mouth. Let him color it! Remember to *talk and let him talk!* He will be learning!

HAPPY HALLOWEEN!

THE BOWDOIN METHOD

PAGE 41

Lesson 36

Christmas Fun

What You Need: Christmas tree and decorations.

Why: To develop many word meanings and understandings. To make your child secure and happy with you.

What You Do: Some of the following may be done with your child.

Put up a Christmas tree. Let your little one help decorate it! There can be so much learning here. "Find me *another red ball* like this one." "Let's put the ball way up *high near* the top." "What shall we put *under* the tree?" "Let's place our *shiny tinsel* around from branch to branch."

Let your child answer your questions as you work. Let him have fun! Teach him word meanings as you talk! This is real learning for your child. Remember, in order to be successful in school, he needs to know *thousands* of meanings of words.

If you make your own decorations, let your child help.

As you walk about the neighborhood, call attention to the Christmas *decorations* . . .

in the stores,
on the streets,
in the windows,
on the doors.

Talk about what they are, their colors, the different kinds.

Let your child watch you as you wrap your *Christmas presents*. Talk about the present, what it is, who it is for, what color it is. Talk about the wrapping paper and the ribbon. Let your child help as much as little hands can!

As you prepare your food for Christmas, remember to talk about what you are doing . . . let your little one watch from a chair. WHAT HAPPY MEMORIES! MERRY CHRISTMAS!

THE BOWDOIN METHOD

Lesson 37

Shoe Box Train

What You Need: A few empty shoe boxes and string.

Why: To teach new word meanings and understandings relating to transportation, to help your child learn through play.

What You Do: Let your child watch (and help cut the string) as you make a *hole* in *each* end of each box. With a *short string* tie each box to the *next* one. Tie a *long piece of string* to the *front box* so your child can *pull* the cars. As you make the train, talk to your child. Tell him what you are doing . . . this is the way your child learns!

Play *Trainman*
Tell your child to be *engineer*.
Ask: "What will you put in the cars?" (Pieces of wood, spools, paper, rags, empty bottles, etc.)

Say: "Now *pull* your train to the *first station*. The *first stop* is *over beside* the bed. The *station* is Nashville, Tennessee.

Now *unload* your train. (Explain.) Take the *empty* train. Where shall we go next? Lets *go* to Sparta, Tennessee. All aboard! Away we go! Now, pull your train to the next stop over by the chair *Load it up again*. Choo! Choo! Toot! Toot! Away you go, Mr. Engineer."

(Encourage your child to play alone after you have shown him how. Teach him to put up his train for another time when he is ready to play again.)

Read this poem. Read it several times. Enjoy it with your child. Your child will catch your enthusiasm!

"Clickety-clack, clickety clack
The train comes down the track!
Ding-ding. Ting-a-ling!
Hear the bells ring!
Chug-chug!
Puff! Puff!
Toot! Toot!
Clickety-clack, clickety clack
The train comes down the track!"

THE BOWDOIN METHOD

Lesson 38

Learning With Boxes

What You Need: Assorted boxes of different sizes. Try to find at least three different size boxes.

Why: To teach your child to think (developing his brain) and to help your child develop new understandings such as big, little, and middle size.

What You Do: Mother, do some of the following:

1. *Thinking skills*—Put three empty boxes before your child, also the box tops, and mix them up. See if your child can find the right top for each box and put the top on the box. COMPLIMENT!

2. *Show Me*—Ask your child:

Show me the box that would be *best* to *use* for shoes.

Show me the box that would be *best* to *use* to put a big bag of potatoes in (or coal, etc.).

Show me the box that would be best for baby's shoes (or your hair ribbons, a watch, etc.).

This will help your child develop his ability to reason.

3. *I Am Thinking*—Play a game, *I Am Thinking*. I see a box that would be *just* the *right size* for a bunny rabbit, some candy, your coat, Jane's doll, your truck, etc.

(See if your child can choose a box that would be suitable for the object. You may have to show your child that the certain box selected may be too big . . . or too little . . . but he needs to learn to think!)

4. *Counting*—Count the boxes. Count the box tops. Count both boxes and box tops. Ask: Which is biggest? Smallest?

5. Play *Which is Gone?* Let your child close his eyes. Remove one of the boxes. Let your child open his eyes and guess which one is gone . . . the *big* one, the *middle size* one, or the *small* one? (This will help develop visual memory.)

6. Read this:

"A *big* box for Daddy's shoes,
A *middle size* box for Mom's,
A *little* box for mine!"

"A big, big box for puppy dog,
A middle size box for my white rabbit,
A tiny little box for the little turtle.
"Big boxes,
Middle size boxes,
Little boxes!"

BE ENTHUSIASTIC, your child will be happy and learn faster!

Lesson 39

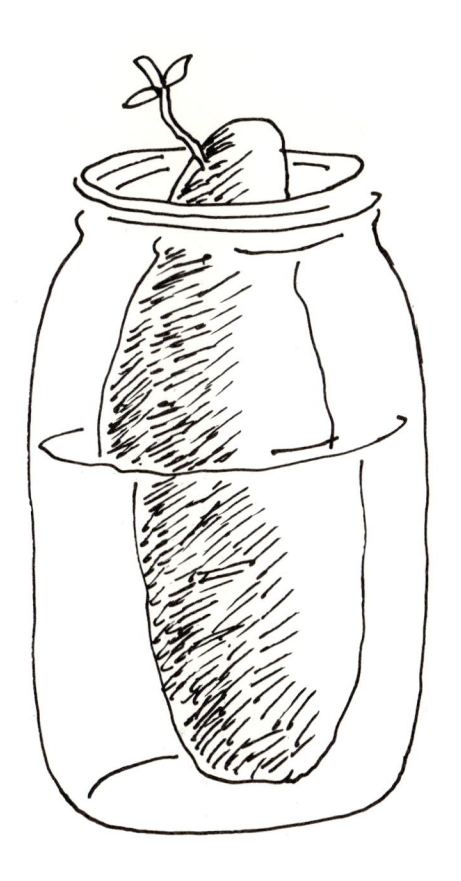

Watch It Grow

What You Need: Potato, jar, water.

Why: To teach your child new word meanings and develop understandings.

What You Do: Get a sweet potato. Tell your child you are going to let him or her grow a *plant*. Explain that plants have to have water. Let him put water in a jar and put the potato part deep into the jar.

Then explain that for a *few days* you will need to *put it away* in a *dark place* (under the sink or in a cupboard). Let your child examine it after a few days and see if it is *sprouting*. Explain that these are little hairy like roots that will help the plant to grow.

Tell your child that when the *plant begins* to grow it *will feed* on the food from the potato. All plants need food, too! *Plants need sunlight* to grow, and *we need to put them in the window*.

In a few days some *tiny little leaves* will *appear* right *on top* and will grow and grow and grow! (Make it interesting . . . watch your child's eyes light up. Talk as you would talk to an adult. Your child will learn more this way.)

Tell your child that this is his plant. It needs *water, sunlight,* and *food* to make it grow. Explain that the potato is the food for the plant. Tell how, when the *farmer* plants potatoes, they are *covered with dirt,* and they grow and make more potatoes under the dirt. They grow under the *soil—* the *ground!* Explain things several ways so your child will learn many word meanings. Remember he should understand 20,000 words and speak at least 3,000. Then the farmer *digs* the potatoes, puts them in *baskets,* and brings them to the *market* for us to buy!

Read this poem several times:
My Potato Plant

"Sometimes in the springtime
When the day is hot.
I get a sweet potato
And put it in a pot.

"I put some water in it
I like to see it sprout.
Some hairy roots go down
And I like to look about!

"I see the tiny leaves
As they appear on top.
They grow and grow and grow.
I think they'll never stop!

"I love my potato plant
With its shiny, green leaves.
If I put it outside
It would dance in the breeze!"

THE BOWDOIN METHOD
PAGE 45

Lesson 40

Teaching With Socks

What You Need: Some socks—a pair or two of different sizes and colors.

Why: To teach many skills—likeness and difference, size and number relationships, colors, visual memory, and things that belong together.

What You Do: There are many lessons you may teach. Some of these are:

1. Put the socks out on the bed or the floor in order that your child may see them well. Ask your child to *find two socks* that *go together*... two that are *alike*. (Have about three socks, one of a *different* color. If he can do this, compliment him; if not, show him the two alike and ask him again after you mix them up.)

2. Say: "Now let's *play a hiding game*. You *close* your *eyes,* and I am going to *take one away*. See if you can *guess which one* I took. Now... remember... no *peeking!*" (If your child can do this, say, "My, how *smart* you are!" Build the feeling that *he can do!* He will learn more easily.)

3. *Count the socks.* Count with your child. "*How many* do we have?"

4. Now ask your child to *take one away* and see *how many are left.* Count with him. ("Yes that's right! Good Boy!")

5. Try to get socks of different sizes. Ask: "Which is the *biggest* sock? Which is the *least* one... the little one? Which sock would be the *right* size for the baby? Which would *fit* big brother? Which would be *your sock?*" (You are teaching your child to think! He is learning how to associate ideas... this is important for developing his intelligence.)

6. Now ask: "What do we do with socks? Why do *we wear them?* Which is the *toe?* The *heel?* What do we do when they wear out?" (Explain that means we get too many holes in them.) "Yes, we have to go to the *store* and *buy* some *more,* and we have to have *money,* don't we? But *we take care* of our socks and try to make them *last a long time.*" (Keep expanding on what you are telling your child. Say it several different ways. This is the way he learns words!)

7. If you have socks of different colors, see if he can find the red sock, the blue sock, the brown sock, etc. (This will help with colors... keep repeating.) "What color socks do you have on?"

If you have time, make a puppet out of a sock by stuffing it and sewing buttons on for eyes and mouth. Make one, and let your child have fun with it!

Mother, your child will be hearing many words in this lesson.

THE BOWDOIN METHOD

Lesson 41

Blowing Bubbles

What You Need: An empty spool and some soap flakes.

Why: To teach your child some new understandings and to give him the warmth and security he needs as he has fun with you!)

What You Do: Let your child watch you as you make your own bubble *blowing mixture by dissolving soap flakes* or *clear bath soap* in *warm* water. Talk as you mix! Your child will learn from hearing and watching you. Talk about whether the water is *hot* or *cold* or *warm* as you work.

If you have some *vegetable coloring*, *a few drops* can produce surprising results! A few drops of glycerine will improve the mixture, but neither of these is necessary!

Give your child an *empty thread spool* to blow the bubbles through. Let him *dip one end* into the soap mixture and blow through the *other end*. A bent wire (making a circle) with a small piece bent as a holder will make larger bubbles.

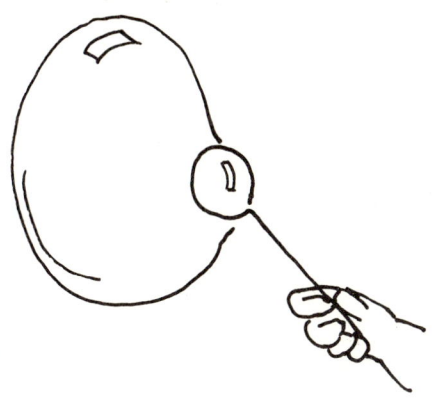

Even larger bubbles can be blown by dipping your child's hands into the soap mixture, *holding them together, palms* up about a *foot* from the *mouth*. Teach him to *blow gently* into the *gap between* his hands. (Did you ever do this when you were a child?)

Count the bubbles . . . one, two, three, four!

Talk about the number of bubbles blown. (Use "Many bubbles," "*few* bubbles" . . . these are two understandings your child needs when he goes to school.)

Let your child *blow up, blow down, blow to the right, blow to the left,* etc.

Let your child watch the bubbles until they *burst.* If you happen to have a piece of wool, your child can keep his bubbles flying by keeping them *in the air* with a *small piece* of the *wool* on a cardboard. He may *chase* the bubbles!

Let your older children play with your little one! HAPPY BUBBLE BLOWING EVERYONE!

Read this poem to your child:
"Bubbles go high
  Up toward the sky.
Pop! Pop! Pop!
  Now they stop!"

THE BOWDOIN METHOD

Lesson 42

Chairs Teach

What You Need: A chair or chairs.

Why: To develop word meanings, number relationships, and likenesses and differences.

What You Do: Mother, ask: What do we *use* a chair for? (Encourage your child to tell you. If your child says, "sitting," say, "Yes, you use a chair to sit in." You are using a complete sentence while he uses one word. Always expand on what your child says by making a complete sentence . . . he learns by hearing you talk.)

How many *legs* does the chair have? *Count with me.* Yes! one, two, three, four! (Let your child count after you.)

Show me the *seat* of the chair. Show me the *back of the* chair. (Compliment if your child knows . . . "My, how smart!")

Tell your child that a chair is made of *wood* which we get from *trees*. It is *furniture*.

Ask: "Do we have another chair like this one? Find it for me."

"Do we have a chair that is *different?*" (Explain what this word means.) "Find *another chair* in the house that is *not like* this one."

"Let's go in the kitchen. How many chairs can you count? Count with me. Are they all *alike?*"

Now, let's play a game! (Make it fun for your child.)

I am going to tell you something to do and *see* if you can do it. Listen carefully (open your ears)! Mother give your child some directions . . . if he does these correctly, always PRAISE!

Children learn by listening and by following directions:
Sit down!
Stand up!
Walk behind the chair.
Stand in front of the chair.
Walk around the chair.

(Give the directions again and see if your child can remember how to do them. Say, "My, what a *good listener* you are! You *followed directions* well." He will not know exactly what you mean, but these are words he will need to understand in school.)

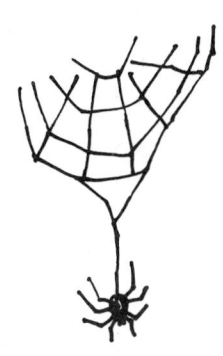

Lesson 43

The Spider's House

What You Need: Look about the house, porch, or yard and see if you can find a spider web.

Why: To develop an interest in nature, to teach your child to observe, and to learn new word meanings.

What You Do: Tell your child these things about a spider:

Tell your child that a *spider spins* his *web* so that he can catch *flies* and *bugs* to eat! In this way he helps us get rid of bugs that might hurt our garden plants. Tell your child that there are *different kinds* and *different colors* of spiders. Some garden spiders are brightly colored. Other spiders are gray or brown. Only *very few* spiders are harmful. (But don't encourage your child to catch one.) Tell your child that a spider makes his web because on the *underside* of his body he has spinnerets. They are *little silk glands* inside his body. When a spider wants to spin a web, he *forces* out *liquid silk* that hardens when it touches the air. He *fastens* the *thread* to a blade of *grass* or the *branch of a tree* and *crosses up and down and back and forth* until his web is finished.

Try hard to find a real *cobweb* and look at it with your child. You will be surprised at how interested your little one will be! He will not understand everything you say, but he will be learning and listening and thinking!

If you or an older child in the family know the song, "The Eensy, Weensy Spider Went Up the Water Spout," sing it or do it as a finger play with your child. What fun for him!

"The eensy, weensy spider went up the water spout! (climb up arm with fingers)

"Down came the rain and washed the spider out! (make hands fall like rain)

"Out came the sun and dried up all the rain! (make sun by holding arms above head)

"And the eensy, weensy spider went up the spout again!" (climb arm with fingers again).

Ask your child to show you how he can play this with his finger.

THE BOWDOIN METHOD

Lesson 44

Talking Pictures

What You Need: Pictures on this page.

Why: To teach the word meanings — spots, light and dark, heavy, big and little. To help your child learn to look at pictures and think! To help your child appreciate differences.

What You Do: First, ask your child to tell you the names of all the pictures. (Go from left to right on each row.)

Talk about: The spots on the animals. (Tell him when the spots are dark or light, large or small.)

The little boy with freckles. (Tell him some people with fair complexion have them.)

Read this Poem:
"There are some spots
On my little face.
Freckles they say
Are all in place.
"They won't wash off.
I try and try,
But my freckles stay there
Even when I cry.
"But Mom likes my
Funny little spots!
My red hair too
She likes just lots!
"My puppy likes them
He has some too!
Do you like spots?
I hope you do!"

(Mother, this will help you build good attitudes about people who are different and who look different. It is good that we teach our little ones that people look different . . . but we like them in spite of being different!)

Play a game: I am thinking of an animal that gives milk, (that has a shell, etc.). Let your child guess what animal you are talking about.

PAGE 50

THE BOWDOIN METHOD

Lesson 45

Something Is Missing

What You Need: Pictures on this page and a crayon or big pencil.

Why: To teach your child to think, to teach him to look for little things. (This develops his visual power which will help when he begins to learn to read.)

What You Do: Show your child each picture. Tell him something is missing . . . something has been left off. See if your child can tell you what it is and ask him to put it on.

Let your child talk about each picture as he works on it. (Let him do it himself.)

Call this game *Sharp Eyes*. Read this poem:

"Look! Look!
With your sharp eyes
What is missing?
Work hard . . . try!

"Is it one hand
With which to eat?
Is it an animal
Without any feet?

"Sharp eyes, sharp eyes
What is wrong?
Look at the picture
What is gone?

"Tell me, tell me true
What is missing?
I need you.
Tell me sharp eyes."

(BE SURE TO COMPLIMENT IF YOUR CHILD CAN SEE THE MISSING PART. HELP HIM IF HE CANNOT. GO OVER THE LESSON AGAIN AT ANOTHER TIME.)

THE BOWDOIN METHOD

Lesson 46

Setting The Table

What You Need: Plate, knife, fork, spoon.

Why: To help your child learn new words and develop his memory and visual perception (remembering what he sees).

What You Do: Mother, your child will be happy helping. Here are several things you may do:

1. If you have dishes that do not break easily, your child can help you set the table. Ask: "*How many plates will we need*... *let's see, one for you,* one for... and one for... etc." Now *count* and see if we have *enough!*

Do the same for the forks and spoons. While you are teaching this, you might as well begin to say and show which goes on the *right* of the plate and which on the *left.* (Your child will not know right and left, but begin to talk about it and show... the knife and spoon at the right of the plate, the fork at the left, the glass at the right near the top of the knife.)

Talk about *setting* the table and help your little one understand what this means. COMPLIMENT FOR HELPING! Talk about *being careful,* not *breaking* anything!

2. Let your child check to see if there are *enough chairs* for all *the family.* (Use these words... he needs to know them when he goes to school.) Count the chairs.

3. Take a knife, fork, and spoon and place them before your child. Ask him to close his *eyes* while you *remove,* take away—use both words—one of the objects. Now let him open his eyes and *see* if he can remember which you took away. If he can remember, COMPLIMENT! If not, try again. Then mix up the objects and remove another. Make it a game! Fun!

4. Take a plate, knife, fork, and spoon and place them on the table. Let your child *see* if he can take the same objects and *place them in the same order, or same pattern* which you have made. Vary this... see if he can copy your pattern. (If he can do this, reading will be easier when he goes to school.)

Examples to try:

5. Talk about the colors of the dishes. If you have different colored plates, your child may pick from three the one that is different.

(Don't be discouraged if your little one cannot make his look exactly like yours; show him; teach him *to look* and *copy yours!* Mother, a few minutes a day and you will be teaching many things!)

THE BOWDOIN METHOD

Chapter 2
HOW TO HELP YOUR CHILD DEVELOP PRE-READING SKILLS

Dear Parent:

This chapter contains six segments. Each segment will help you teach a different skill which will help your child learn to read. They are all important to your child's success when he is given his very first book.

The segments are:
1. **What is Missing?**
2. **Did you Listen?**
3. **Which are Alike?**
4. **Which is the Right Picture?**
5. **What Does Not Belong?**
6. **What Happened?**

Learning to read is a hard task for many children. You can help make it easier. Use the directions in this chapter carefully. Use the segments for which your child seems ready! DO NOT PUSH! THIS WILL DO HARM!

Always COMPLIMENT your child for correct responses. Be PATIENT when he needs help. USE FOR ONLY A FEW MINUTES — AND WHEN YOUR CHILD IS INTERESTED. When you have done this, your child will have developed most of the pre-reading skills important for success in reading.

Happy Teaching!

Ruth Bowdoin

1. WHAT IS MISSING?

These pictures will help you or someone in your family teach your child **something very important.** It is a skill that he will need to develop in order to learn to read.

Using this part of the book with your child will help him develop in two ways: (1) his ability to **look carefully** (this is called **visual skill**) and (2) his ability to **think carefully** and to **talk** with you.

Use it occasionally before your child goes to kindergarten, during kindergarten and first grade. Work just a few minutes! Even five minutes will mean much!

MAKE LEARNING FUN! Give much **PRAISE,** make your child feel important.

1. Here is a toy to play with. What is it? What is missing from the wagon?

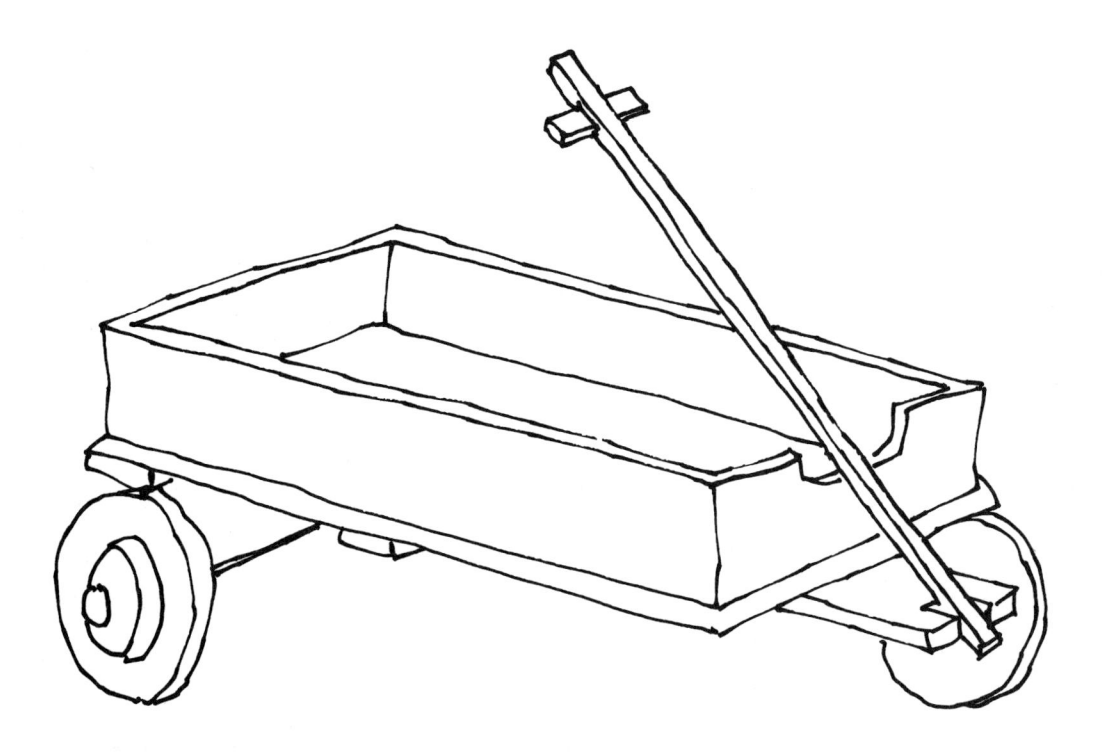

2. What animal is this? What is missing from the picture? What does the elephant need in order to be complete? *(Talk in adult terms. This is how your child learns.)*

3. Here is a kitten licking his milk. What is missing from his body? *(You may need to tell your child — his tail.)*

THE BOWDOIN METHOD

4. Here is a person. What is missing?

5. Here is a rooster. What does he say? What is missing?

PAGE 56

THE BOWDOIN METHOD

6. Here is a piece of clothing. What is it? *(Yes — a jacket, a coat.)*
   What is missing?

7. What is this girl doing? *(Yes, she is kicking a ball.)* What is missing? *(Yes, her foot.)*

THE BOWDOIN METHOD

8. What is this? *(Talk about a clock telling time — show the numerals. You may have to tell your child the long and short hands are missing. Show him on your clock at home.)*

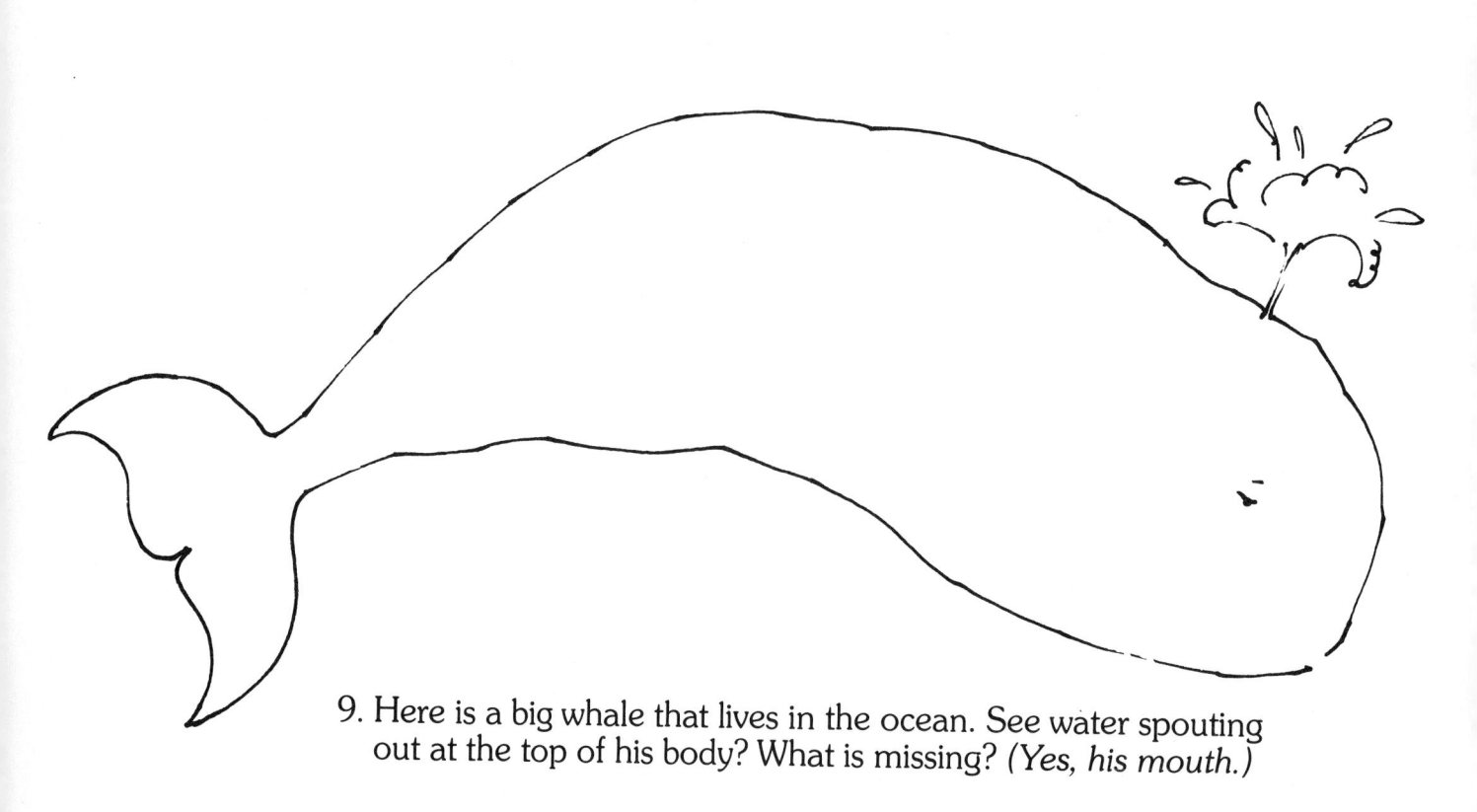

9. Here is a big whale that lives in the ocean. See water spouting out at the top of his body? What is missing? *(Yes, his mouth.)*

10. Look at the truck. It is used for transportation. *(Use big words.)* What is missing? What is gone? *(Praise your child if he can show you.)*

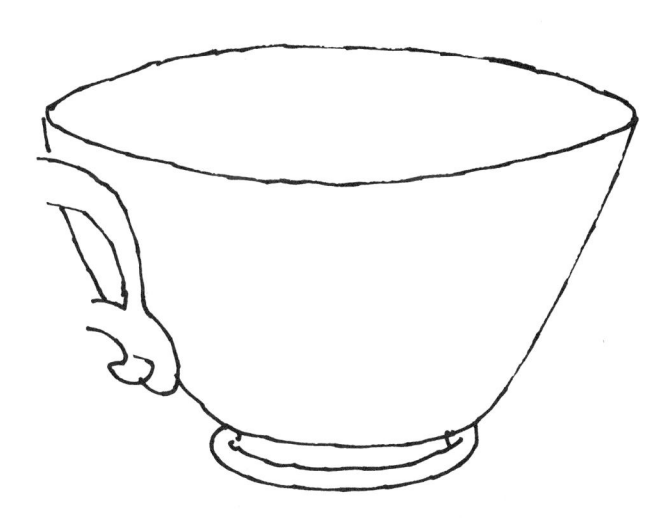

11. What is this? What is missing? *(Praise your child. Say, "Handle — yes, the handle is missing.")*

THE BOWDOIN METHOD

12. See the house. What is missing?

13. What is this *vehicle? (Use big words.)* Yes, it is a school bus! It carries passengers to school. What is missing? *(You may need to help your child see that there is no door.)*

14. Here is a duck. What does he say? What is missing?

---

15. Here is a funny face. What is missing? *(Yes, he needs another eye. Where does it go? PRAISE.)*

2. DID YOU LISTEN?

Listening is a skill. Your child will do better in school if he learns to develop this skill. This part of the book will **help him learn to listen and to think** as he listens!

When your child begins first grade, his teacher will be testing his ability to listen by using little short stories and pictures. Let him do this with you. **GIVE HIM A HEAD START! YOU WILL BE GLAD YOU DID!**

1. Mother had so many things to do. The clothes were ready to be ironed. She needed to do some sewing. But the children were very hungry. What do you think mother would use first? *(Mother, this may be hard for your child. Explain kindly.)*

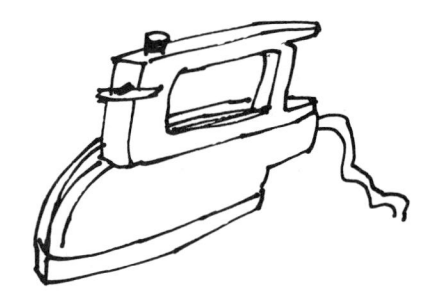

2. Father needed to paint the cottage (the house). But first he needed to cut the grass. What would he use? *(If your child does not get the right answer the first time, read it again.)*

PAGE 62 THE BOWDOIN METHOD

3. John was very hungry. "May I have an ice cream cone", he asked. "I think fruit would be better for you to eat. It is almost time for dinner." What did John eat?

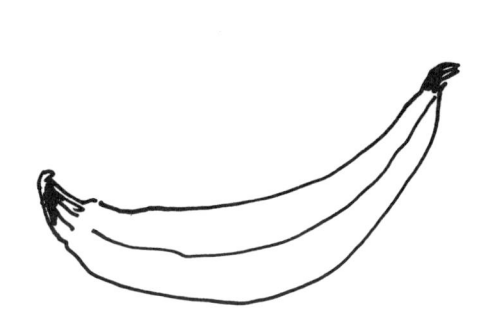

4. It had been snowing very hard. Father had shoveled the snow from the walk. It was dark and he could not see how to get to the car. What would he use?

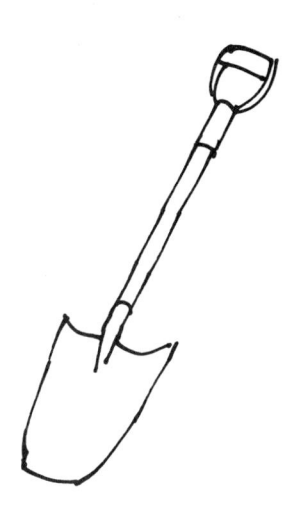

5. Grandmother was coming. Alice wanted to surprise her. Father said she could paint a picture. Mother thought she should color with her crayons. Johnny said she could cut out some paper dolls. She wanted to do what Johnny said. What would she use?

THE BOWDOIN METHOD

6. Father wanted to get some wood to burn in the fireplace. He needed enough to last through the winter. What would he ride in to get the wood? *(Mother, this may be hard…Explain. You are teaching your child to THINK!)*

7. Mother wanted to hear some soft music. No one could blow the horn. The radio was broken. But she did have a record player. What would she use?

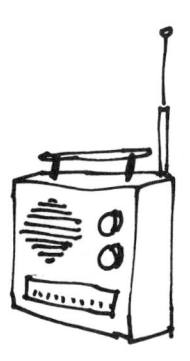

8. It was time to eat. Mary was a big girl. Burt was a little boy. Susie was a little baby. What milk would Susie drink? *(If your child gets the wrong answer the first time, read it again.)*

PAGE 64   THE BOWDOIN METHOD

9. Father needed to make a trip. He had to get there in a hurry. What would he ride in?

10. Father went to the barn to feed the hungry animal. Show me the picture of the animal he would feed. *(Praise for correct answer.)*

11. Mother was very busy preparing dinner for her family. What would she use in the kitchen?

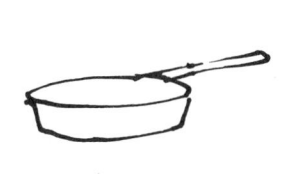

THE BOWDOIN METHOD

PAGE 65

12. Mother called to Susie, "Come in the house and let me get you ready to have your long hair cut off." Which picture is Susie?
   (Explain if your child does not know.)

13. Tommy's cat was cold and hungry. After he had fed him, where did Tommy take his cat to make him warm? *(Compliment your child if he knows.)*

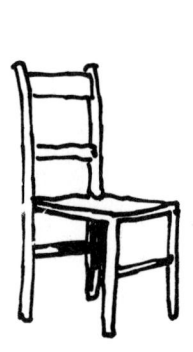

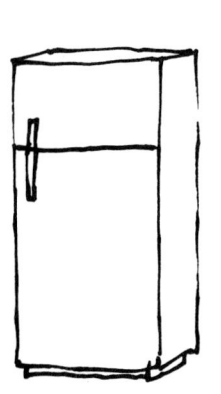

14. Up, up, up! Mother bird stretched her wings and flew away to find food for her baby. Show this picture to me. *(If your child shows you the wrong picture, read again and point to the one flying.)*

15. Mary's mother wanted to get up early to take some pictures with her new camera. She is afraid that she will sleep too late. What does she use to help her wake up? *(Your child may show you the camera. Explain patiently that she used this to take the picture. But what does she use to help her wake up?)*

---

16. Father needs to build a house for Spot. He needs to drive the nails. What would he use?

---

17. Something is wrong and mother is calling for help. Show me the picture.

THE BOWDOIN METHOD

3. WHICH ARE ALIKE?

This chapter is to help you teach your child a very important skill . . . the ability to see things that are **alike** and things that are **different.**

When a child enters school, he will need to learn to see likenesses or differences in letters and words. But first, he needs to have lots of experience in seeing pictures that are alike or different.

Ask your child to tell you **why** the picture is different. Do not tire your child . . . use the book only for a few minutes.

PRAISE your child when he is successful—make him feel good about what he can do!

1. Which two girls look *alike?* Which one is *different?*

2. Which two strawberries are *just alike?*

PAGE 68

THE BOWDOIN METHOD

3. Show me the two dogs that are *just alike*. Now, show me the dog that is *different*.

4. Which two shapes are *alike?*

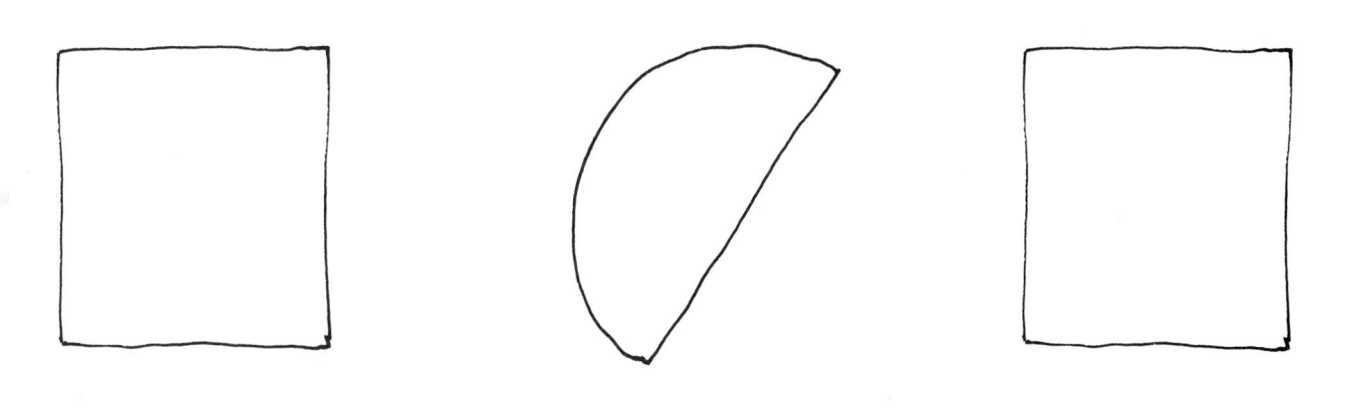

5. Which duck is *different?* Why is he different?

THE BOWDOIN METHOD

PAGE 69

6. Which two are *alike?*

7. Which two are *just alike?*

8. Show me the one that is *different.*

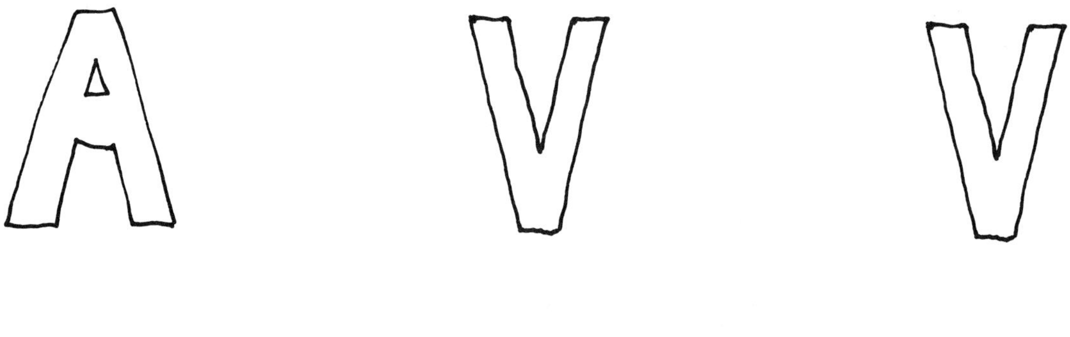

PAGE 70

THE BOWDOIN METHOD

9. Which two are *alike*? How is one of them *different*?

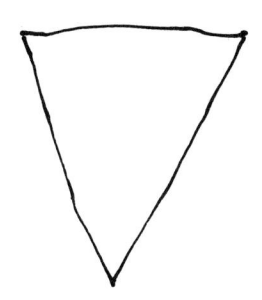

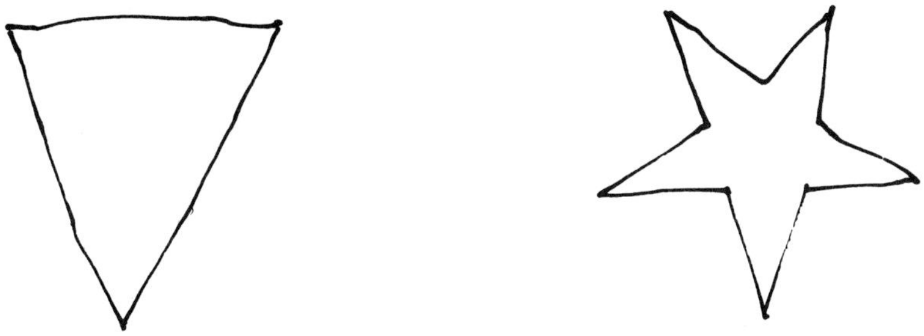

10. Which are *alike*? Which one is *different*?

11. Which leaf is *different*?

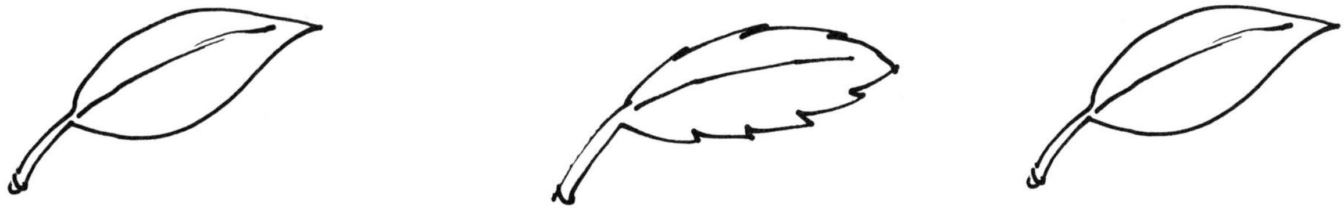

THE BOWDOIN METHOD

12. Which letters are *just alike?* Which one is *different?*

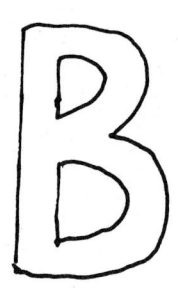

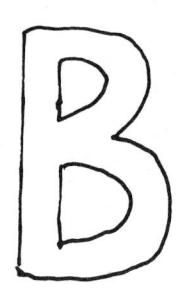

B B D

13. Which nail is *different?*

14. Which two seashells are *alike?*

THE BOWDOIN METHOD

15. Show me the *different* coathanger.

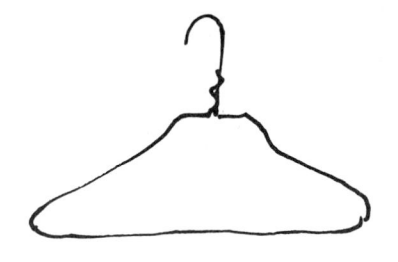

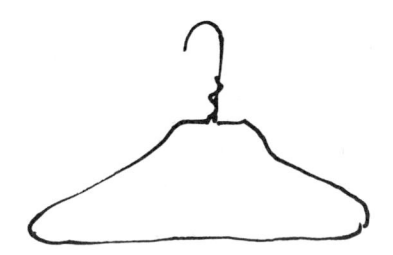

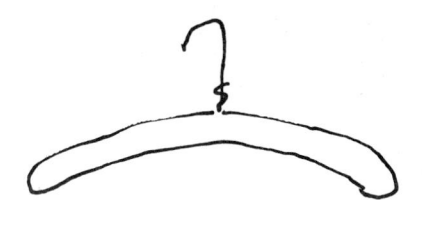

16. Which candles are *alike?*

17. Find the two sweaters that are *just alike.*

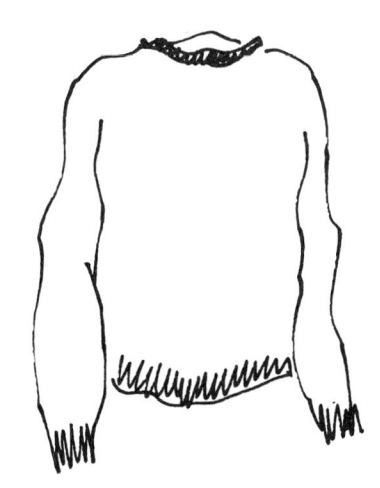

THE BOWDOIN METHOD

4. WHICH IS THE RIGHT PICTURE?

This chapter will also help you develop visual skills. It is a little harder than the section before this one.

Your child needs to do these before he is ready to read. Let him look at the first picture and find another in the **row** just like it. If he cannot find the picture, **help him.** If he can find it, **give him praise!** Use only for a few minutes and do not tire your child.

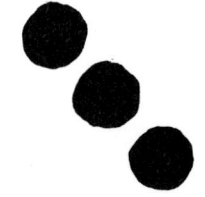

Look at this picture.   Find one just like it here.

Look at this picture. Find one just like it here.

THE BOWDOIN METHOD

PAGE 75

Look at this picture.   Find one just like it here.

PAGE 76   THE BOWDOIN METHOD

Look at this picture. Find one just like it here.

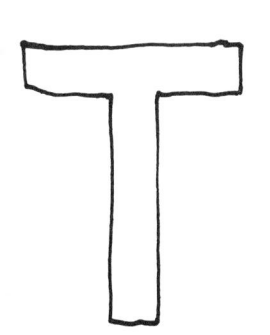

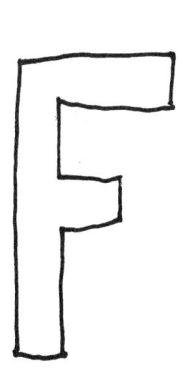

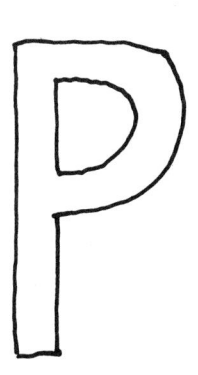

THE BOWDOIN METHOD

PAGE 77

5. WHAT DOES NOT BELONG?

Before your child learns to read in school he will need first to be able to think—to pick out things that go together because they are alike or because they belong to the same group (clothing, toys, people.)

This part of the book will help you teach this important skill.

You will be **teaching your child to think!**

You will be **helping his brain develop!**

You will be **helping him have a more successful start in the first grade!**

Use it only for a short period.

Keep it and use it over and over!

Your child learns from repeating things.

BE PATIENT—MAKE LEARNING FUN!

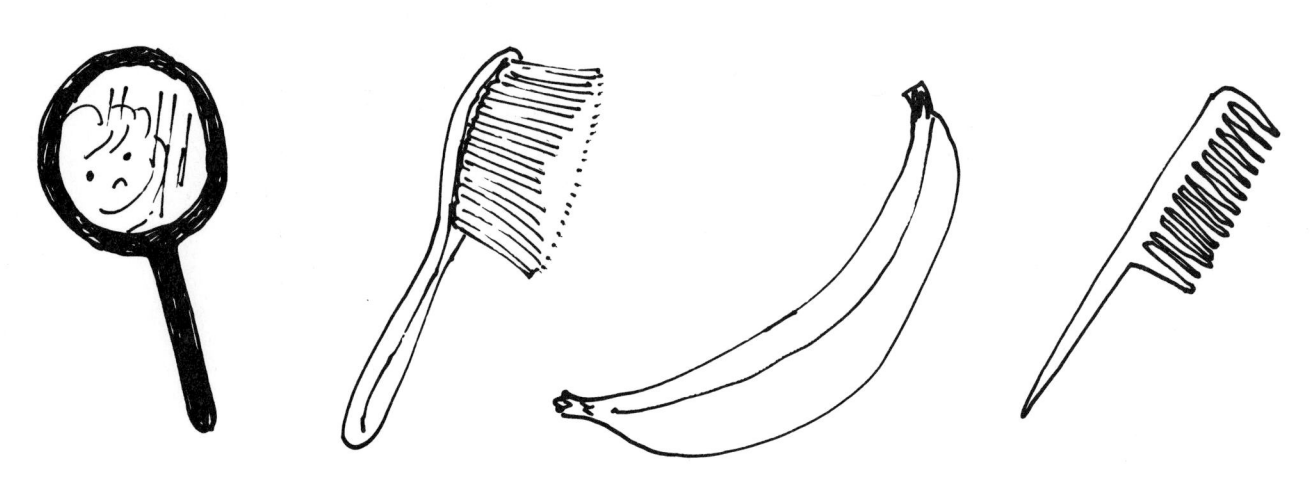

1. The banana. It is used for eating. Others are for grooming.

2. All are clothing, except the block. You cannot wear it!

THE BOWDOIN METHOD

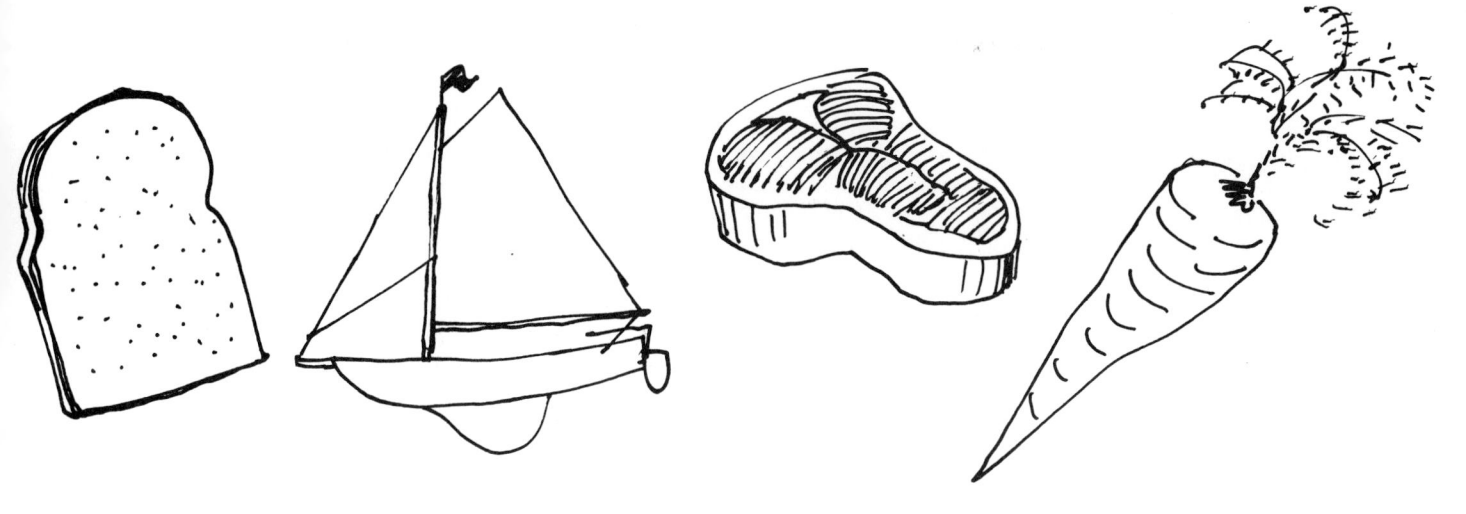

3. All are foods, except the sailboat. *(PRAISE YOUR CHILD FOR THE CORRECT RESPONSE.)*

4. Yes! All are animals, except one — the hammer.

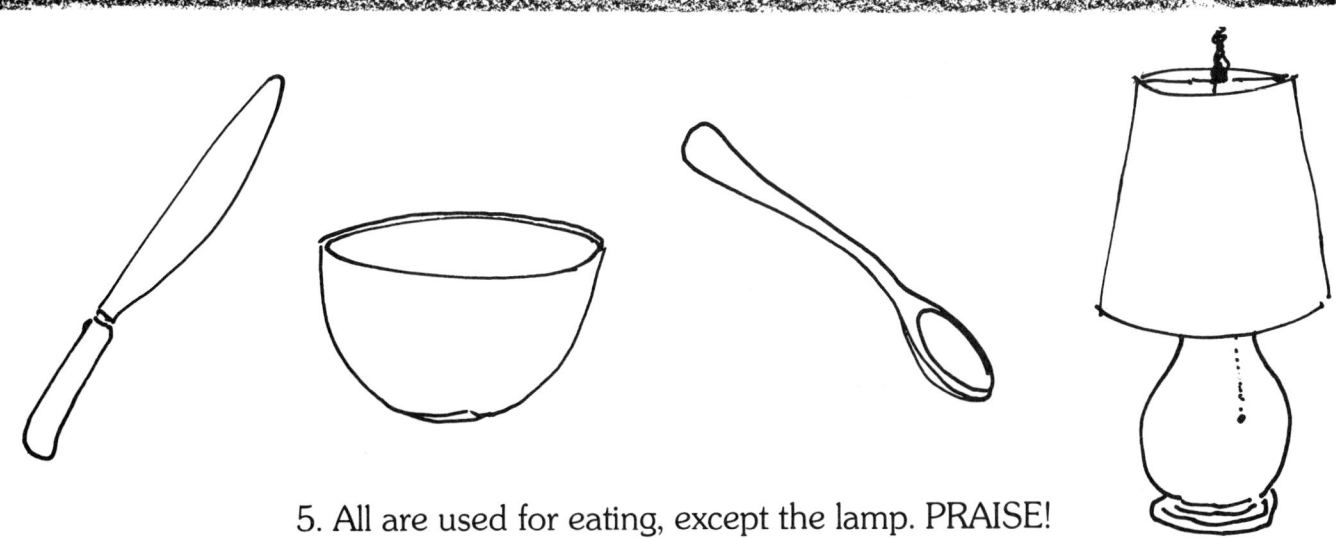

5. All are used for eating, except the lamp. PRAISE!

THE BOWDOIN METHOD

WHAT DOES NOT BELONG?

6. Yes! All are children (persons), except the duck. What is it?

7. All are foods, except the star.

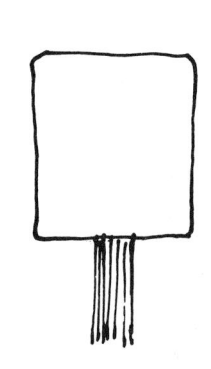

8. All of the signs have letters on them, except one.

THE BOWDOIN METHOD

9. All are flowers. The duck is not a flower.

10. Yes! The monkey is not a person. Talk in complete sentences. This will help your child.

11. The airplane is not clothing. Help your child to understand. This may be hard for him or her.

THE BOWDOIN METHOD

PAGE 81

WHAT DOES NOT BELONG?

12. The screwdriver is not a toy.

13. Right! The jack-o-lantern is not an animal.

14. Yes! All are tricycles, except the saw.

THE BOWDOIN METHOD

15. A tomato is not a bird. So it doesn't belong.

16. All the hats are on men, except one. It doesn't belong. Explain this to your child.

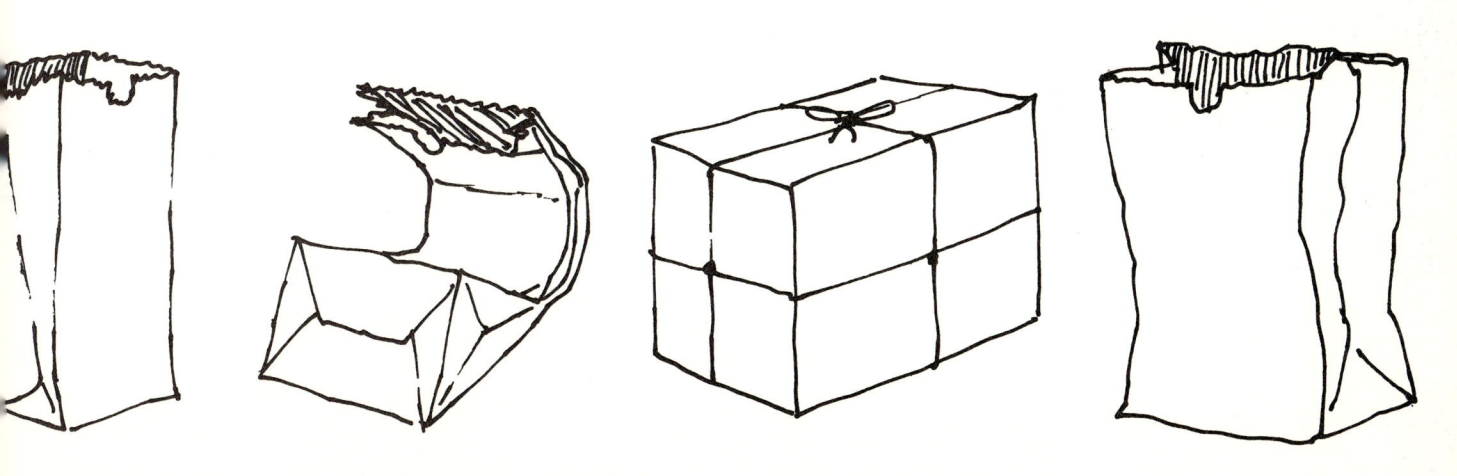

17. The box doesn't belong because it is not a sack.

THE BOWDOIN METHOD　　　　　　　　　　　　　　　　　　　　PAGE 83

6. WHAT HAPPENED?

This chapter will help your child learn to think! He needs this thinking skill before he learns to read. If you use it wisely you will be able to help your child with this skill ("sequence")

On each page ask your child:
WHAT DO YOU THINK HAPPENED **FIRST?**
NOW WHAT HAPPENED **SECOND** (OR **NEXT**)?
WHAT DO YOU THINK HAPPENED **LAST OF ALL?**
BE SURE TO **PRAISE** YOUR CHILD FOR CORRECT ANSWERS! If your child does not know, TELL HIM. MAKE IT A HAPPY EXPERIENCE. HELP YOUR CHILD KNOW THAT LEARNING CAN BE FUN!

What happened **first?**
What happened **next?**
What happened **last?**

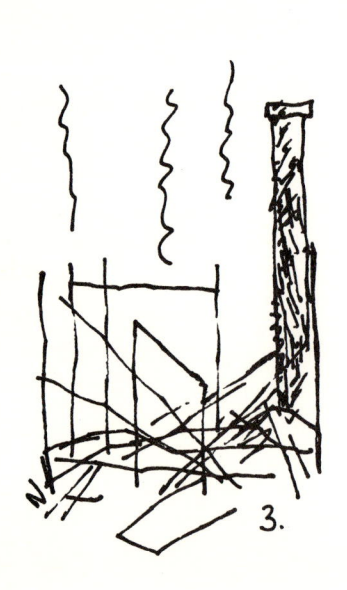

THE BOWDOIN METHOD

PAGE 85

What happened FIRST?
What happened NEXT?
What happened LAST?

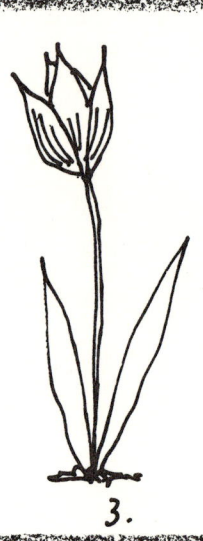

PAGE 86

THE BOWDOIN METHOD

THE BOWDOIN METHOD PAGE 87

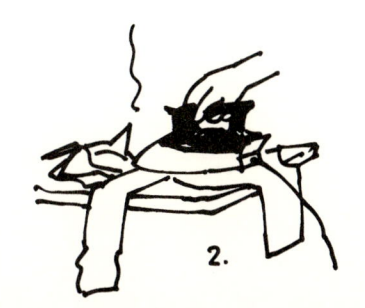

What happened FIRST?
What happened NEXT?
What happened LAST?

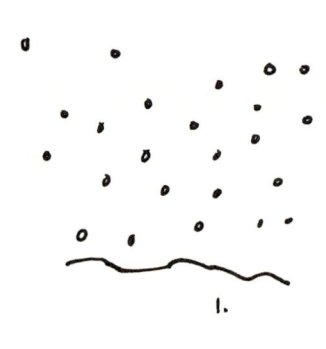

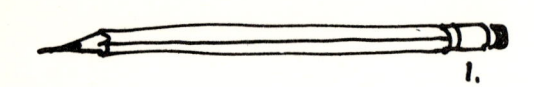

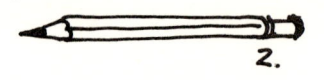

PAGE 88

THE BOWDOIN METHOD

Chapter 3
HOW TO TEACH YOUR CHILD WORD MEANINGS

Dear Parent:

Can you read this?

volpəʌɾr

Well, how did you get along? Can you read this? No?

This is exactly how your child will feel when he gets to school and is given printed matter if he hasn't first had the language and understandings! This is why your child needs to know the meanings of thousands of words.

The development of your child's language and understanding is closely related to the development of his BRAIN.

Did you know that many people believe half of all growth in human intelligence takes place before your child is four years old? Yes! And another 30 percent occurs between the ages of four and eight.

That says something to us all! It tells us that two-thirds of your child's intellectual development happens BEFORE he starts to school!

Please study this chapter carefully (especially mothers and fathers of preschool children). There are many important things mentioned which will help you develop many word meanings and understandings.

This is considered to be the MOST IMPORTANT thing you can do to help your child get ready for the hard job of LEARNING TO READ.

Happy Teaching!

Ruth Bowdoin

Don't worry!

Your child's brain develops very fast between the ages of two and four. This is an important time for him to learn—and he can do a lot of it, with your help and understanding.

But don't panic. All children are different. Speech doesn't develop at the same speed all the time. And some children learn to talk later than others. There may be several weeks or months of difference between the learning of one child and another.

So be patient. And every day try to do some of the things in this book. Worrying will do more harm than good. Just keep working with your child and giving him encouragement as he learns at his own speed.

Why Read?

Studies show that this will help your child become successful in school. Parents who read aloud to small children usually find that their children have fewer problems in learning to read.

Your child will get to know that reading is fun! If you are enthusiastic about the book, your child will "catch" your feelings and will learn that reading is fun. Your child will like to hear you laugh at the funny parts and experience with them the joy of the story!

Your child will get many new understandings and word meanings. Of course the more you read the more word meanings your child will learn. Children in today's world need to know so many things. And many of these come naturally through hearing books read.

Your little one will learn to sit still and listen. This is important. When your child is in school, he will need to be able to sit still for a few minutes. You will be preparing him for this when you read aloud. Compliment him after he's listened to you for awhile. Say, "My, how nice you listened!"

Your child will develop values. Through reading aloud you may help your child develop good thoughts and good attitudes. Ask questions about the story which will make him think good thoughts and develop good character traits.

"Was Mary a nice girl?"
"Would you like to have Sammy for your friend?"
"Wasn't Jane's mother a nice mother?"
"I know Mary must like John for helping her find the lost kitten". All such questions help your child make judgements and develop character and good citizenship.

Your child will learn from the pictures. He will learn to look at and enjoy them. His language will develop if you allow him to talk about what he sees. By doing this, your child will improve his ability to see and think and talk.

You will help your child learn to think. Since your child was born with a brain which develops more rapidly during the early years reading aloud to your child will help him learn to think. This is especially true when you follow up with questions such as:

"Could this really happen?"
"What do you think happens next in the story?"
"Could you tell me about the story?"
"What part did you like best about the story?"
"Who were the people we read about?"

Your child will know you care. He will feel the warmth of your arms. He will know the feeling of being somebody special to get this attention. Your child needs this feeling. It is just as important to his total emotional growth as food is to his physical growth.

Read—Then Read Some More

Begin early.

Read to your child as soon as he can focus his eyes on the pictures in the story.

Make reading exciting! Change your voice when each character speaks. Make your child feel that reading is talking.

When he is old enough, let your child sit and enjoy the pictures. Perhaps you will sit on the side of the bed and read just before he goes to sleep....

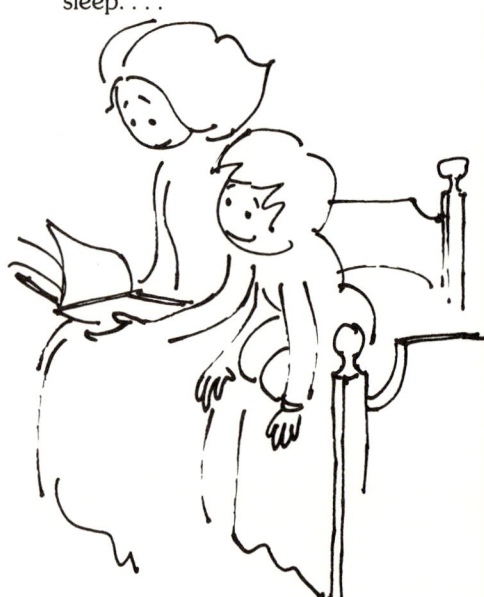

THE BOWDOIN METHOD

Good Words

To do well in the first grade, your child should be able to speak clearly about 3,000 words. Some children, in fact, know as many as 6,000 by the time they become first graders.

That's a lot of words. Luckily, mothers and fathers are excellent teachers. And what's even better is how quickly children can learn new words.

During a child's first year, he will learn to say about three words—words like "Ma-ma," "Da-da," or "Bow-wow." But by the time he's two years old, he can speak about 270 or more words. As the child learns to walk, his word-learning may slow down for a little while. Not for long, though. Soon he should be learning about 600 or more new words a year. If he watches a lot of television, he will probably learn even more.

Of course, your child understands more words than he can speak— maybe as many as 20,000 to 40,000 by the time he is six years old!

The good thing about knowing so many words is that the more he knows the better he will probably do in school. In fact, language seems to be the main thing which helps a child learn to read.

This book will tell you how to help him learn more words.

The way you feel about your reading is important.

Your child will **like** books and want to read them if you help by saying simple things like:

"My, what a nice book!"

"I wonder what our story will be about?"

"I can hardly wait to read this pretty book."

"**Your** book! Let's look at the nice pictures and see what it is about."

These are little things. But they are important. If your child likes to hear you read, he will probably become a better reader in school.

Let Older Children Read To Younger Brothers Or Sisters

How nice it is for an older child to read to a younger one! It will be good for both of them.

It will give the older child a chance to practice his reading and to be the shining star.

Encourage him to read. The more he practices, the better reader he will become. Make it a special privilege for him. Praise him for helping you. Both your older and younger children will profit from this.

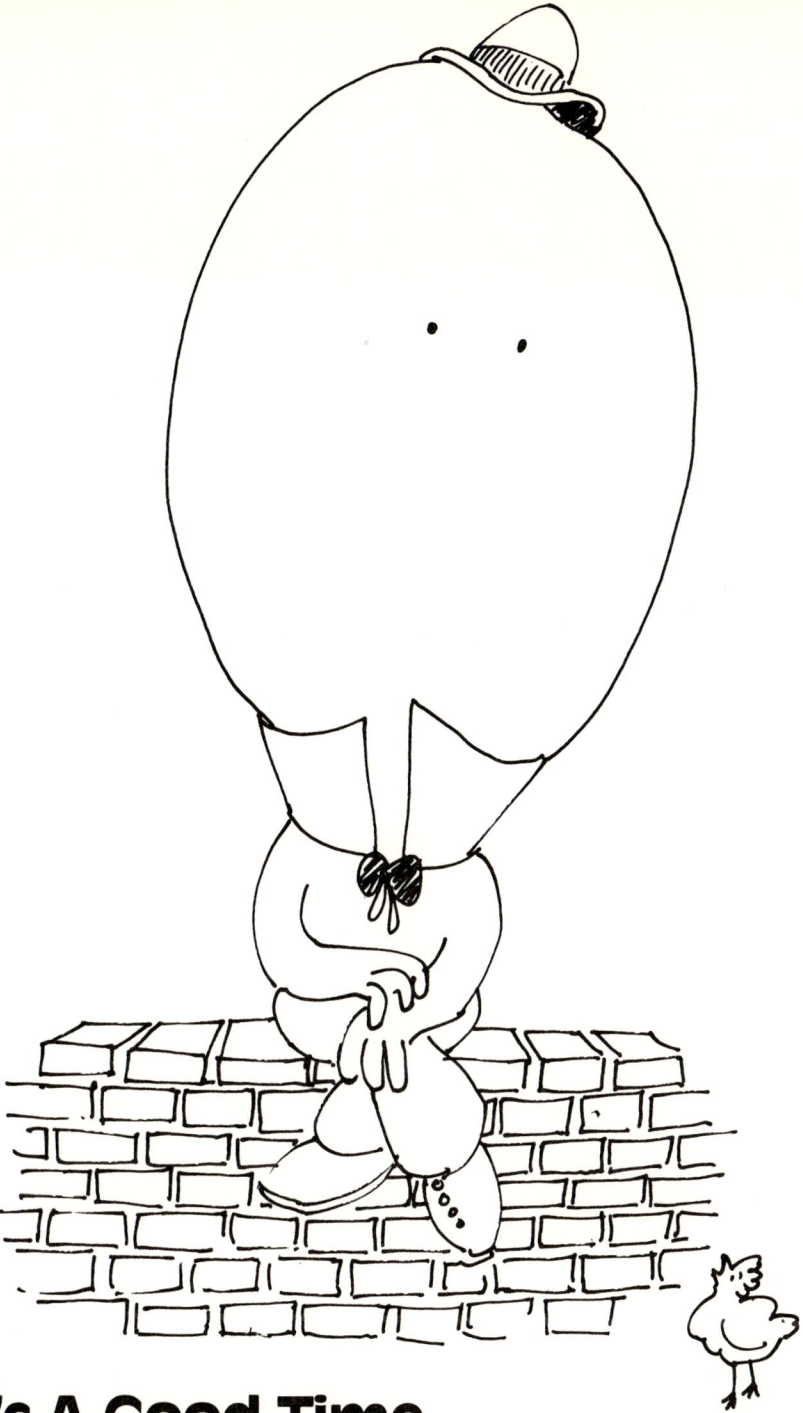

Now's A Good Time For Nursery Rhymes

Do you remember some nursery rhymes that you learned as a child?

If you do, say some of them to your child. Start doing this early—at least by the time he is nine months old. And you can begin when he's even younger.

From these little poems your child will learn sounds and rhyming words. This will help him begin reading when he goes to school.

Read happily! Make it fun. Let your child say nursery rhymes with you. Some nursery rhymes you may remember are:

Humpty Dumpty
Jack and Jill
Baa, Baa, Black Sheep
Hey, Diddle, Diddle
Little Bo-Peep
Hickory, Dickory, Dock

Ask questions about the rhymes. Help your child learn to think.

THE BOWDOIN METHOD

Talk To Your Child

Talk. Talk. Talk.

Your child learns thousands of words by hearing you talk.

Tell your child about simple things in the yard—ants crawling, butterflies flying, bees buzzing, leaves falling, rabbits hopping, and birds singing. Your yard is filled with things to learn about.

Talk about yourself, your family, and your friends. But talk "adult" talk—**not baby talk.** When your child talks baby talk, don't correct him. Just set a good example. "Here's a pitcher," your child may say. "Yes, it's a beautiful picture you drew for me." That's being a good model. And your child learns from this.

Don't talk down to your child. Use the right words—even if they are big ones. You will be surprised how easily your child will begin to understand.

THE BOWDOIN METHOD

"Read" Pictures

Your child learns many things by looking at pictures. Give him magazines or catalogs you may have at home. Use pictures in the books you read to him.

Let him talk to you about the pictures. Help him learn to name the things in the pictures. Talk about the colors in the pictures, too.

If there is action in the picture, get your child to tell you what is happening. Ask questions which will cause your child to think—such as:

What's happening in the picture?

Do you think the weather is cold or hot? Why?

Would you like to have these children as your friends?

Which is the biggest child? Which is the smallest?

Count with me. How many pictures of people are on this page?

Picture reading is a skill. It is taught to beginners before they learn printed words. The more pictures your child "reads," the more likely he will be ready for being taught to read.

Let Your Child Learn Language By Playing

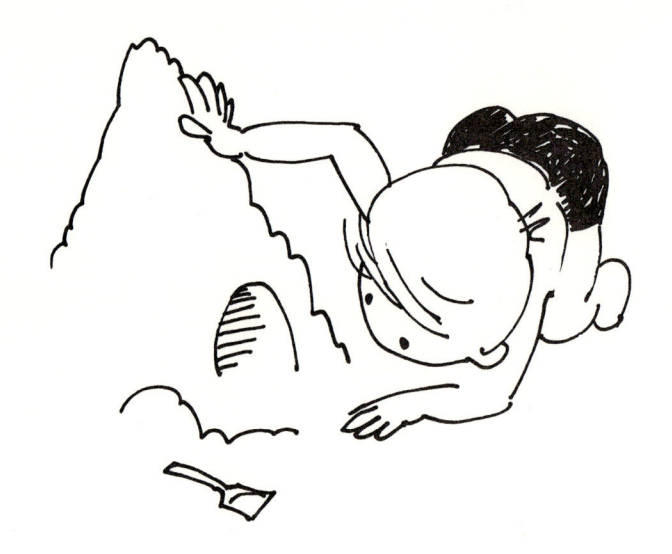

It's natural for your child to like to play. Play is very important. Through play, your child learns many new words and develops many understandings.

He learns by playing with toys. But he learns, also, by playing with pots and pans, spools, sand and water, and things that do not cost money. Not only will he learn about things — how they look and feel — but he will develop his muscles, both indoors and out. Believe it or not, these muscles help him to read.

Encourage your child to play with other children, with you, and by himself. It's fun for your child if you play the customer at his grocery store or the doctor when his baby is sick. When your child plays alone, encourage him to talk to the baby doll or the teddy bear.

Let Your Child Watch Television

Many good television programs are made especially for children the age of yours. They are produced to help your child have fun while learning.

What can your child learn from these and other programs?

Word meanings — many, many of them. And, remember, the more words your child understands, the better reader he probably will be.

About many new things. He will learn about numbers, letters, people, objects, and things to do. This exposure to new things will help your child do well early in school.

Develop other ways of looking at himself and the rest of the world.

Reasons for liking himself. As your child learns more, he will be more pleased with himself and, so, like himself better. He will watch television and think or say or feel, "I can do that" or "I know that."

It is best not to force your child to watch something just because you feel it is educational. This will not be necessary if you encourage by asking questions, talking about the funny characters and what they are doing or saying, following the program with nice comments about how much fun it was. If your child feels that you are having fun, he will have fun, too!

Teach Your Child The Colors

When children start to school, they will be more successful if they know their colors. Let it come naturally.

Talk about the color of the child's sweaters, socks, and shoes. What colors, you can ask, are the foods on the table, signs on the highways, houses along the road, and cars passing by?

Let your child match colors. **Mix up several pairs of socks.** Pick up one and see if your child can find another like it.

Let your child match the clothes he wears—blouse with skirt or shirt with pants.

Take advantage of every opportunity to talk about colors. This will help your child get off to a good start in school.

"Tell Me About Your Picture"

If a child draws or paints a picture, a wise parent will say, "Tell me about your picture." This will encourage the child to talk, to say something, to express himself.

Maybe you're thinking, "What in the world is that?" But you wouldn't dare ask! He may have made a boat—and you thought it was an airplane. What a sad mistake you would have made.

Be happy to accept a scribble! After all, your child's muscles may not be developed. He may not be able to stay within lines. Use the picture to help develop your child's vocabulary and make him feel good about what he has done.

As your child grows older, you may hear "Mom, draw me a pig." Say, "I like the pigs **you** draw."

"I can't," he replies. "Oh yes, you can. Show me."

Accept your child's picture as it is. **Young children should not be shown how to draw.** They do not need to feel that they must live up to adult standards.

THE BOWDOIN METHOD

PAGE 97

Be A Good Example

Yes, Mom and Dad, your children learn from you both. They learn by imitating. They like to watch you and do as you do.

When they hear you say, "Thank you," "Please," "Excuse me," and "I'm sorry," they will learn to say them also.

When they understand the meanings of these words, they will imitate the examples you set and those set by other older people, like their big brothers or sisters.

Your children will develop a feeling for others when they see you and hear you. They may hear you say, "Is that a fair thing to do?" "Would you like to have someone else do this to you?" "We must be kind to the baby— our baby."

You are the example in the development of your children's speech. They need to hear you talk in complete sentences. They need to hear you say long, long sentences. They enjoy having a conversation with you.

This is one way children develop language. This will help them learn to read easier.

THE BOWDOIN METHOD

Do Finger Plays

Your child will have fun while learning language if he is encouraged to use his hands and fingers.

You may remember some finger plays you learned while you were a child.

Did your mother ever play with your toes or your fingers and say

"This little pig went to market.

This little pig stayed home.

This little pig had roast beef.

This little pig had none.

And this little pig said, 'wee, wee, wee,'

All the way home."

Try using your child's toes with this rhyme. Watch him smile.

Your older children may know some of these finger plays and teach them to your little one:

Ball For Baby
The Turtle
Open Them, Shut Them
The Beehive
The Apple Tree
Peas Porridge Hot
Here's A Little Tea Pot
Eency Weency Spider

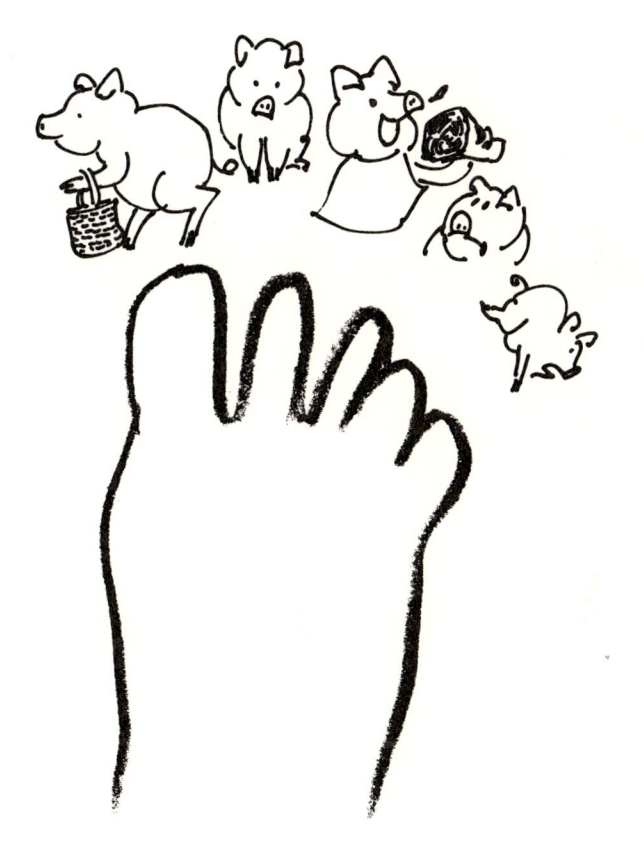

Encourage Questions

"I can't stand it another minute! Just one more question and I'll scream!" Did you ever think that? Or say it? Most of us have.

Still, your little one has so much to learn. And asking questions is one way of learning. Be very pleased if your child asks questions. This shows that he is smart and wants to know things. **Some three-year-olds have been known to ask 300 questions in one day!** Think of how much they learn if only a few of these questions are answered.

"Oh, I don't know what makes the stars twinkle. Stop asking such stupid things."

How does this make your child feel? Hurt. When he is insulted like this, he will probably stop asking.

Sure you don't know all the answers. But you can always say, "That's a really good question. I'm glad you want to know. But I just don't know the answer."

If you have any books in your home which will help with the answer or an older child in school, you may also say, "Let's try to find out. Maybe Johnny can help find out at school."

Your child may ask the same questions over and over. And you will no doubt get tired of answering. **Just remember that your child learns when you repeat.** If you remember this, it will keep your blood pressure from rising!

Encourage Your Child To Pretend

Your child begins to have an active imagination at an early age. All children like to play grown up. Encourage yours to. He can imagine many things and learn from this. He will like to pretend he is someone else, like a doctor, policeman, teacher, mommy, or daddy.

Give your child an old hat, an old purse, or a spoon. Let him "make out like" he is grown up. Encourage him to talk, to make believe. Your child will learn the meanings of many words as you help him play and pretend.

Remember, also, that he is imitative. Encourage him to be kind, thoughtful, and courteous. He will catch these from us adults.

Respect Your Child's Imaginary Friends

"You can't play with my dog," you may hear your child say. You stop and listen, and you are amazed. There is no one around, and your child doesn't even have a dog.

There are many reasons why the young child plays make-believe with an imaginary friend. His imaginary friend may help him deal with feelings that he has. Or he may simply be lonely for the friendship of other children.

Some good things can come from this. By talking with his imaginary friend, he develops his language, and this is much better than his being alone. He will outgrow his make-believe friend when he has some of his own and when other members of his family talk with him.

Don't worry if your young child talks to himself. You may even need to cooperate with him in this make-believe experience.

Stretch Your Child's Sentences

"See car," your child says.

"Yes, I see that beautiful, shiny, green car with the black hard top, traveling at a fast speed, past the houses and the buildings as it goes down the road."

What have you done? You have accepted your child's two-word sentence, and you have stretched it into about 25 words!

Will he understand what you say?

Of course not.

But he will begin to understand many of the things you say as you develop the habit of making your child's little sentences into big ones. He will learn more word meanings than you can ever imagine.

Besides, your child will know that you respect what he says, that you hear him, and that you care.

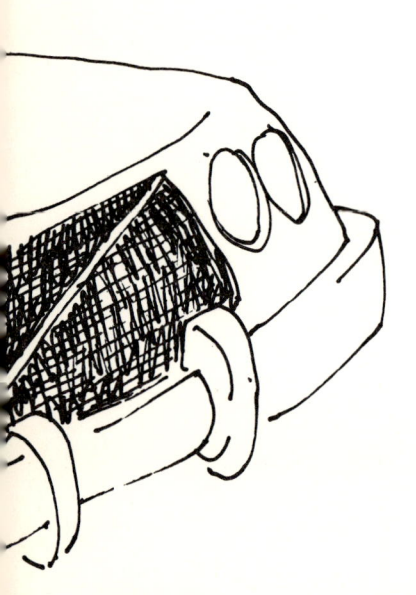

Walk Into Words

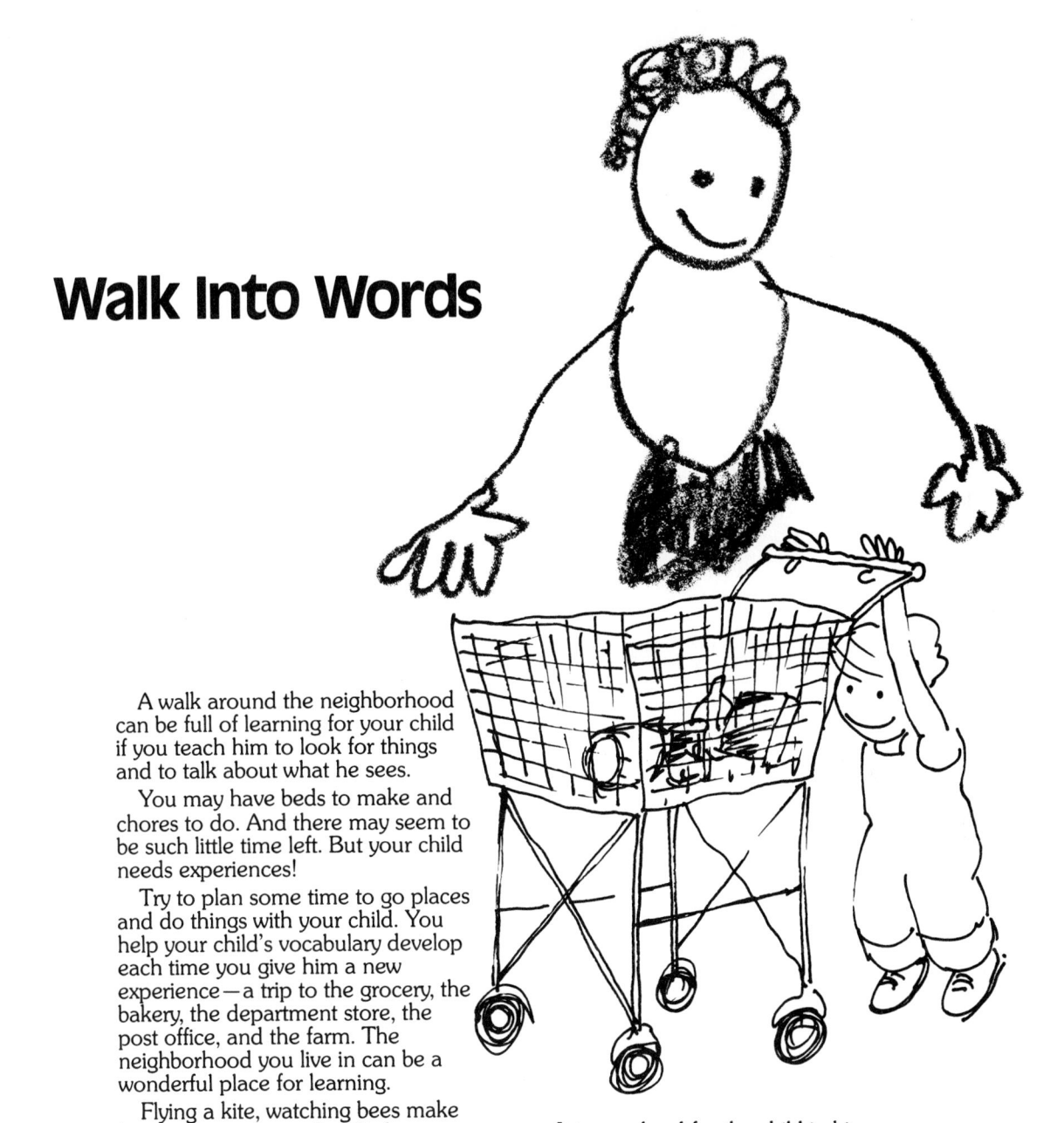

A walk around the neighborhood can be full of learning for your child if you teach him to look for things and to talk about what he sees.

You may have beds to make and chores to do. And there may seem to be such little time left. But your child needs experiences!

Try to plan some time to go places and do things with your child. You help your child's vocabulary develop each time you give him a new experience—a trip to the grocery, the bakery, the department store, the post office, and the farm. The neighborhood you live in can be a wonderful place for learning.

Flying a kite, watching bees make honey, seeing butterflies flit from flower to flower, watching a mother and father bird build a nest, and picking up leaves will give your child a background for reading.

It is very hard for the child in his early reading to read about something he has never seen or heard about. **Do things with your child!** This will help his brain develop.

Use Nature To Help

Our children develop their word understandings by looking and observing. They need us to show them many things.

"Look at the pretty green leaves on the plant. Do you know what made this plant? Well, we planted a little seed, and inside this seed was a baby plant. We put it in the soil, watered it, and set it in the sunshine. Pop, pop! Soon the baby plant began to push its way out of the ground. Look at its leaves. One, two, three green leaves."

When we talk with children about using things in their surroundings, we are teaching them many things which will help them become good students in school. They will be learning new words and developing new understandings. They will be learning to notice things about them and to appreciate them.

Your child may become one of the children who takes the teacher a bunch of wildflowers or who gets excited about the first robin he sees hopping around. Then your child will be learning about the world and its wonders.

Give Spoken Directions

Teach word meanings by giving your child simple directions.

Start with **one thing,** such as, "Go to the door," or "Put your hand on your head," or "Walk to the kitchen."

After your child understands one simple direction, **add another.** "Go to the door and touch it," or "Put your hand on your head—then on your nose."

A little later, **add three directions.** "Go to the door, touch it, and come back and sit on my lap."

Remember to **praise** your child when he listens and follows your directions. This will help him learn, and he needs to feel important.

Begin with one direction, then two, and finally three. **But make it a happy time!**

You may be surprised how many word meanings your child will pick up—**and how fast!**

Sing And Listen To Records

Your child can gain many new word meanings and understandings through singing songs and playing records.

He learns the meanings of new words while he responds to the rhythm of the music—clapping and moving his body. And he will also learn to love music.

Check your television schedule for music programs for young children. Encourage your child to sing the songs he learns in school. Talk about them. Let your child know you believe this is all important. **It's true!** And it will make him happy.

Let Your Child Try

Yes, of course, it's easier to do a job yourself. But look how much learning your child will miss.

It may be a simple thing, like helping with the dishes or sweeping the floor. But your child will be "helping Mom" or "helping Dad." **He will feel important and useful.** This is good. It's a feeling we all need.

Or it may mean that your child just holds the pan while you put in the biscuits or cookies. Maybe he watches while you are mixing, rolling, cutting, and baking. But you're doing more than this. **You're talking and explaining what you're doing.**

Use your work to help you teach your child word meanings. He needs to know thousands of words before he enters school.

Most of all, these experiences with you will give your child a happy feeling of belonging, sharing, and loving.

Let Your Child Think

Does your child have many opportunities to think for himself?

Just as we need tools for our garden, our child needs tools to help him learn to think. In school, the teacher will say, "Think now...." If your child has developed the tools for thinking, he will be able to "Think now...."

What are some of these tools? One of the most important ones is language. The many word meanings your child knows will help him develop his thinking ability. **He cannot think without knowing words!**

He needs to have had a lot of experiences to have a background for thinking. If the story he is reading is about a clam or an apartment building—and if he has never seen one or a picture of one—he would have trouble thinking about them. Many children say words well in reading, but saying words is **not** reading. **Reading is thinking!** Ask good questions. Help your child learn to think!

Teach Your Child To Understand Numbers

One ball.
One, two, three balls.

Help your child learn the meaning of numbers.

Let him count the people at the table, plates on the table, chairs in the room, beds in the house, or objects in a picture.

Ask, "How many are there? How many more do we need?"

Talk about **big and little, large and small, long and short, many and few, top and bottom, heavy and light.**

"Should I Teach The ABC's"

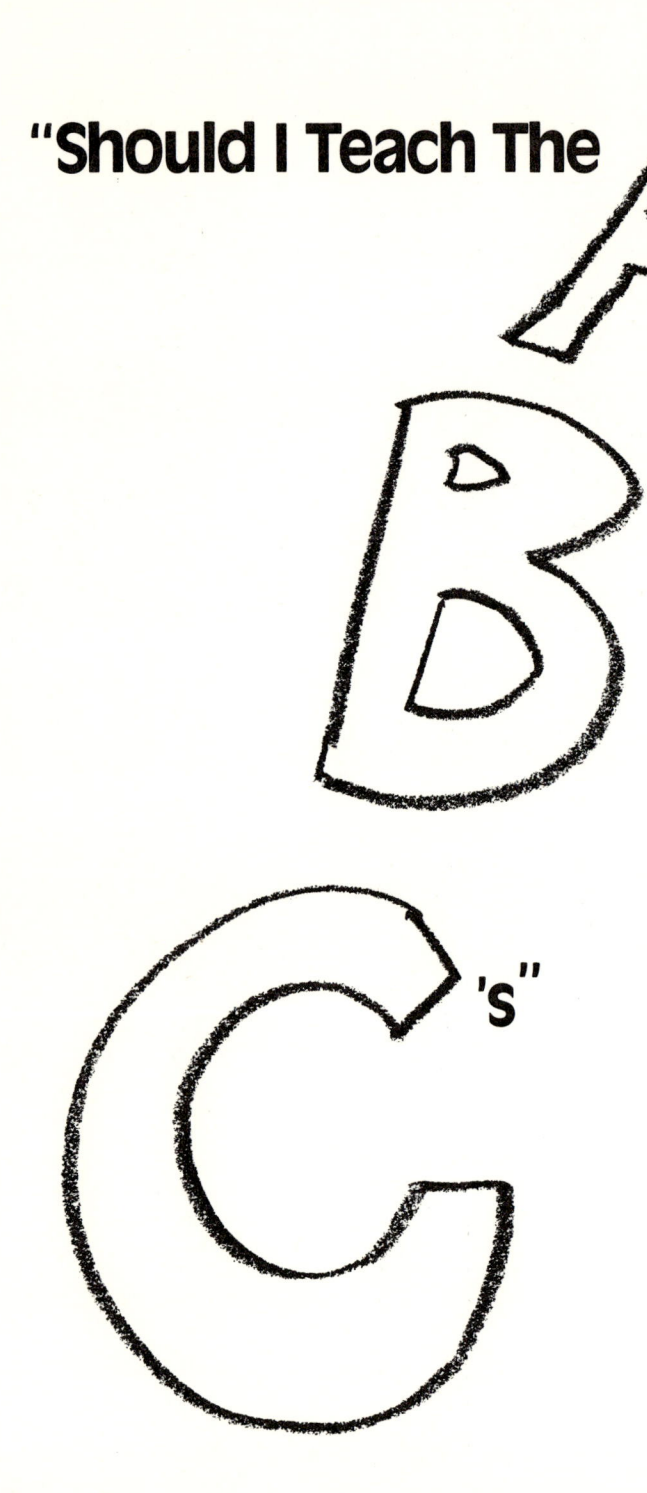

This is a question many parents ask before their child goes to school. The answer is "Yes"—**if your child is interested.** If your child asks you the name of a letter, tell him.

But don't drill and worry yourself or your child while trying to teach the letters.

There are other things more important to your child's early learning than this. It is more important, for example, for your child to be able to:

talk in complete sentences

express himself clearly

understand the meanings of many words

love books

It will not hurt your child to learn his abc's. It may even help **if** you make the learning pleasant and happy—with no pressure. The **Sesame Street** television program teaches the alphabet in a pleasant way.

All of your child is involved

You are fooling yourself if you think you can teach your child language and understandings separate from other things. Each child is a whole. We can't separate language from life. **All** of your child is important—how he feels about you as a parent, how he feels about himself as a person, how he feels about those around him. This is his emotional makeup and is important to his learning.

And there is the physical. The hard-of-hearing, the child who may have trouble seeing or walking, the child who is not eating properly or feeling tried or sick can't develop language and understandings with as much ease as other children may be able to do.

Your child wants to grow. You want to help. But you do not want to push. A beautiful flower does not grow without good soil, water and sunshine. Your child does not unfold like a flower! **His language does not develop without some help from you, the parent! A**s long as you use the opportunities provided you in your daily living—and these are mentioned in this book—good things can happen to your child which will be a big help in his being successful when he begins to read!

NOTES

PARENT ACTIVITIES FOR HOW TO TEACH YOUR CHILD WORD MEANINGS

Activity One — Unscramble These Letters

Unscramble these letters. They will spell words which tell ways of helping your child learn many word meanings. These are necessary for learning to read well. A space indicates more than one word.

        C P E I N X R E E S E _____
        I R P U S C E T _____
        V E T O L I S E I N _____
        S O T U S I Q N E _____
        L D D I E R S _____
        T A U D L - T K L A _____ _____

Activity Two — Picture Reading

When your child is very young, point to a picture and say "Tell me what this is." If your child knows the object, compliment. If not, say the word immediately.

Later as your child begins to develop his/her vocabulary, talk in more detail about the pictures. You may use a child's book (inexpensive one may be purchased). Say something like this:

"Tell me about the picture." (Encourage your child to see and talk about several things in the picture.)

Then ask specific questions requiring your child to think. For example, "Do you know what color the little boy's shirt is?" "What is he doing?" "Do you think you would like him for a playmate?" "Why?"

Picture reading is *very* important in preparing your child for the complex skill of learning to read! The more words your child understands, the better chance she/he will have to be successful in reading. Don't miss this opportunity!

Activity Three — Using Your Book

Underline:

Three things you may say in order to help your child learn to like books. (P 91)

Two advantages of the older child reading to the younger. (P 92)

Nine things you may talk to your child about while she/he learns new word meanings. (P 94)

Eight things parents may do to encourage a child who is watching a good television program. (P 96)

Three reasons why a wise parent who can't identify the child's picture says "Tell me about it!" (P 97)

Some of the natural ways you may teach your child the colors. (P 97)

The names of the finger plays you know that you could teach your child. Add any others to the list which you may know. (P 99)

A good response if you don't know the answer to your child's question. (P 100)

Three things you teach your child by using nature to help. (P 104)

Three things that are more important to your child's early learning than drilling on the alphabet. (P 110)

Activity Four — Dialogue

Listen to the conversation between mother and Justin. List all the ways mother used to develop his word meanings.

Mother: Would you like to help me sort the clothes? Get all the towels for our first wash. Tell me the color when you put them in the machine.
(Mother helps with the colors.)
My! What a good helper you are!
When I put in the washing powder and turn on the machine, we'll read a good story!

Justin: I'll get the book! (He gets the book.)

Mother: You selected a good one! (Mother encourages Justin to talk about the pictures.)

Mother: Now I must answer Aunt Martha's letter. Would you like to make a picture? We will send it to her with your message.

Justin: Uh huh. Let me get my colors. (He scribbles a picture.)

Mother: Now tell me what you want me to say to Aunt Martha and I'll write it on the picture. (Justin obliges and mother compliments.)

Justin: I'll play with my truck.

Mother: Good! Haul some blocks to Mr. Smith to use to repair his house. He needs lots and lots. Deliver them to his house and stack them neatly.

(Justin begins to play.)

Mother: I'll call you when Mr. Rogers comes on TV.

What methods did Mother use to develop lots of word meanings?

_____   _____

_____   _____

_____   _____

(Did you find as many as six ways mother used?)

Activity 5 — How Do You Measure Yourself In Teaching Word Meanings?

(Circle Yes or No)

Do you ____

Yes	No	Usually read to your child daily?
Yes	No	Encourage older children to read to your young child?
Yes	No	Make listening to books fun for your child?
Yes	No	Take time to talk about the pictures?
Yes	No	Say nursery rhymes?
Yes	No	Talk to your child while you work?
Yes	No	Encourage good television?
Yes	No	Stretch your child's sentences?
Yes	No	Encourage good thinking?
Yes	No	Help with learning A, B, C's (if your child is interested)?
Yes	No	Do finger plays?

Do you ____

Yes	No	Teach your child colors in a natural way?
Yes	No	Encourage pretend games?
Yes	No	Encourage talking about pictures your child makes?
Yes	No	Encourage your child to ask questions?
Yes	No	Give your child experiences with things and people?
Yes	No	Use things in your surroundings to teach?
Yes	No	Let your child help, even if it is easier to do it yourself?
Yes	No	Help your child learn number understandings (not just the name of the symbol)?

(Work on your "No" answers.)

Activity Six — Singing Vocabulary

As your child "acts" out words, sing to the tune of "Here We Go Round the Mulberry Bush." Use lots of interesting things. Take into consideration the age and development of your child.

> This is the way we build a house,
> build a house, build a house,
> This is the way we build a house
> Early in the morning."

(Drive the nails, lay the bricks, paint the walls, climb a ladder, make a garden, cook our dinner, etc.)

Have you done this?   Yes   No

"A Visit To The Grocery"

If either parent has the time, a trip to the grocery can be a fine place for teaching a wealth of word meanings. If your child is old enough, you will be able to compare sizes of cans. "Let's get the BIGGEST can of tomatoes." "Help me find the SHORT box of shredded wheat." "We need a GALLON of milk." "It is on the BOTTOM shelf. Get it for me."

You will need to establish guidelines before taking the trip in order that it will be pleasurable. For example, "You may select only <u>one</u> thing to buy for yourself!" Have your list ready in order to keep down the "Mamma buy . . . ." problem!

I have made the grocery a learning experience for my child.
☐ occasionally   ☐ many times   ☐ not at all
☐ I plan to do this.

"Take a Neighborhood Trip"

Take your child on a trip around the neighborhood. Lots of learning can take place in your yard and neighborhood. Carry a paper bag. Help your child find things to put in the bag — rocks, leaves, blades of grass, clover, wildflowers, sticks. Talk about each thing that your child puts in the bag. When you are back home, talk about these again. More talk . . . more word meanings!

* * * * * * * *

Activity Seven — Games

"Guess What It Is?"

Put a few objects in a box. Let your child close his/her eyes and select one of the objects. See if the object can be identified by feel. If not, you describe it and let your child guess! Don't forget to compliment!

Have you done this?   Yes   No

* * * * * * * *

"Thinking Sound Words"

These words will help your child associate sounds made with objects. Say: "Let's play a game. I'll say a sound-word and you tell me what makes the sound." Then say such words as the following:

jingle-jangle	fizz	sh, sh
buzz-buzz	zoom	woof-woof
tick-tock	drip	quack-quack
pop	bang	bow-wow

Have you done this?   Yes   No

Activity Eight — Filling In Blanks

1. Between the years _____ and _____ your child's brain develops very fast.

2. To do well in first grade, your child needs to be able to speak about _____ words and to understand as many as _____ or more.

3. _____ seems to be the main thing which contributes to a child's learning to read.

4. After learning to walk, a child learns _____ or more new words each year.

5. Parents who read aloud to small children usually find that their children have fewer _____ in reading.

6. A wise parent will begin to say nursery rhymes to the child by the time she/he is _____ old.

7. Ask questions about pictures which will enable your child to _____.

8. You are the _____ in the development of your child's speech.

9. Respect your child's imaginary _____.

10. Stretch your child's _____.

(Check your answers by looking on pages 90, 91, 93, 95, 98, 101 and 102.)

THE BOWDOIN METHOD

REMEMBER . . .

- Your child deserves the support system given by your positive words.

- Words that build negative feelings are harmful to your child and to you.

- "Good words" make both you and your child feel better.

- Memorize some positive words and make them a part of your everyday life. You will be surprised at what they can do!

- The early years are the most important years of your child's life.

- Just as your child needs food, there are emotional needs which must be met if success is attained in school and in life.

- If your child consistently feels "My mommy and/or my daddy like me" she/he is on the way toward a healthy launching!

- Your child needs to feel good about himself/herself, good about others and be able to learn with ease and happiness.

- Mental illness can be prevented if parents and teachers help provide for the eight basic needs discussed in this book.

- Language is important in learning to read.

- Reading to your child and making the reading experience a happy one should be a parent's primary goal.

- Using "adult talk" with your child enhances language success.

- Play is important in developing language.

- You can help your child learn many new word meanings in very simple ways which take very little time.

- The more experiences a child has, the richer the background for learning new word meanings.

- You are your child's first and most important teacher!

* * * * * * * * * *

Share this book with all caregivers — grandparents, baby sitters, day care workers, and others who "touch" the lives of your children."

Chapter 4

HOW TO HELP YOUR CHILD DEVELOP EMOTIONALLY

Dear Parent:

Do you want your child to grow up to have a healthy personality? Of course you do. We all do.

This chapter contains EIGHT things which your child needs in order to develop his or her emotional needs. A good parent will work toward trying to meet these needs. While your child's needs may, and often do, differ from those of other children who may be the same age, most people agree that ALL CHILDREN EVERYWHERE need to have the needs met that are in this book.

If these needs are met at A VERY EARLY AGE you will find that your child should feel good about himself, good about others, and be able to learn with much greater ease and happiness.

Many people today are mentally ill, or have many personal problems. Many of these problems could have been avoided if parents had started early and had provided for these basic needs.

Happy Teaching!

Ruth Bowdoin

LOVE

My mommy likes me!
She says I matter very much to her.
Sometimes she kisses me.
She sits close and holds me tight.
"I couldn't do without you," she says to me.
My mommy loves me!

How Do I Show My Love?

I tell him with my TOUCH

My arms are there when he needs comfort. My fingers gently rub the little stubbed toe or the wounded knee. My hands dry the tears away when he is cross or unhappy. My lap holds him when he is sleepy or tired, and when I read to him.

I tell him with my FACE

This is not always easy. But I try. He looks at my frowns and my eyes as they dart angrily here and there when things don't go well with me. And he feels this. So I smile a lot. This helps. He knows I'm happy.

I tell him with the SOUND OF MY VOICE

I try to make it soft and pleasant. But there are times I would like to shout out threats. I have found it's better to keep my voice low, maybe in a kind of whisper. Things seem to go better in my home when I do this. Better for me. Better for my child.

I tell him with my WORDS

I sometimes say "I love you". But my child knows I do not need to TELL him. He FEELS it in his heart! And this may be the most important thing I can ever give him. But I remember love is not to spoil. And love can't be bought! I may give THINGS but THINGS are not LOVE. And giving things is not giving love.

Yes, my child knows that he is loved. He knows by the things I say, the way I look, the tone of my voice, and the way I act.

THE BOWDOIN METHOD

ACCEPTANCE

My mommy likes me just the way I am.
She isn't always saying, "I wish you could be like Jimmy".
And she doesn't care if I grow tall like my daddy so I can play basketball.
She likes me just the way I am.
And she likes me ALL THE TIME.
When she gets all tired and out-of-sorts she never says I drive her crazy!
She does tell me she doesn't like the way I act.
But she NEVER says she doesn't like me!

Why Does My Child Feel This Way About Me?

I accept my child for being himself

I know that his ears are big . . . too big for his face and they droop over a bit, especially when he wears his grandpa's straw hat! He is too little for his age. I DID want him to grow to be tall. But I would never let him know I felt this way.

He's my third boy and we wanted a little girl! But these are things I can't change. His father wishes he had one basketball "star" in the family. But I keep telling him our child needs to be WHAT HE IS . . . NOT WHAT WE WISH HE WERE!

I can't let him do as he pleases, but I can be fair

Sometimes it would make me feel good to 'beat him up', especially when he acts bad before company. But if I did that it would only hurt us both.

Yes, I accept my son with his big, floppy ears and even his naughty behavior. But I will work toward making him better.

I understand that there are some things he can do well, and some that will be hard.

This I know.
I accept this, too.

SECURITY

My mommy lets me hold her hand when I need to.
She says "Don't be afraid. I am here. I will not let
anything hurt you".
She wants me to know that she is near and cares what happens to me.
When my mommy leaves, she says, "I'll be back soon.
Don't worry if I'm not at home.
Somebody will be here".
My mommy wants me to know that home is a good, safe
place to be and that someone is close by to help me if I need it.

How Do I Give My Child This Feeling Of Security?

I begin early
I give my child as many new experiences as I can. The more he sees and does, the more secure he will be. I encourage play with other children and take him places where he will see different people.

I prepare my child when he has to face something new or strange
"Will it hurt Mommy?", he asks when we start to the doctor or the dentist. I answer the question truthfully, "Of course it may hurt just a little, but not for long".

"But I don't want to go . . .", says my child. And I tell him firmly, gently, lovingly . . . "But you MUST!" He has no choice. This gives him security.

I never shame
Sometimes things frighten my child. But I never shame him for being afraid. I hold him. I explain to him. I let him cry without trying to make him stop. I try always to think that there is a CAUSE for all behavior.

I don't threaten unless I mean to carry it out
I never tell my child if he doesn't behave I will give him away, or that I may go away and leave and not come back. These can be real bad ways of hurting! And I do not want my child to hurt. I always tell my child when I leave home. I never slip away.

I don't want to overprotect
To do this may cause my child to be too dependent upon me. Then he will be afraid to leave me. If he is secure, he will be able to turn me loose! He will be able to walk out the door and enter school or enter into a new experience with his head held high! "Goodbye Mom", he can say with assurance.

CONTROL

"No," my mommy says gently.
"No, I'm sorry. You can not do that!"
She lets me know there are things I may not do.
But she doesn't say "NO" all the time.
She is kind to me.
She tells me to play quietly when the baby is asleep,
to take care of toys because they are expensive,
to listen because it is a polite thing to do.
She doesn't fuss and fight and "storm out" at me!
Sometimes she may punish me if I hurt someone.
She says, "You may have bad feelings, but I won't let you hurt others".
But I know she loves me, even if she has to punish.

How Do I Control My Child?

I try to teach "self-control"
As soon as my child is old enough to understand I use the word "control". Control of the hands when he hits or snatches. Control of the mouth when he bites or spits. Control of the feet when he kicks. Control of the voice when he shouts. Control of his words when he talks!

I try to be a good example
Sometimes I lose my temper. I don't always feel like having patience. But when this happens, I try to remember to tell my child "I am sorry. I was not kind. It is my fault. Things have not been good for me today and I guess I am taking it out on you!" Surprising how well this works. I need to explain. This helps my child respect me.

I understand your feelings
I explain that it is all right to get angry or to feel bad inside as long as he does not "take it out" on someone else. It is his behavior that is BAD. He can correct that.

I believe my child will be what I THINK HIM TO BE.

I set limits early
I teach my child that there are things that he must not do. And I do not allow him to do as he pleases. But I must stick to this *every day*.

I am firm but never harsh
I know that my child really likes to have fair rules to live by. Even my older children like to have these rules too.

I tell my child WHY
But my very young child may not really understand. I tell him anyway. Soon he will get to know that I have a reason. "You can't do that because. . . ." Then he gets to understand (although he may not like it.) When he is older he will respect me for it.

THE BOWDOIN METHOD

PAGE 125

GUIDANCE

My mommy knows I need friendly help in growing up.
She knows I really want help.
She helps me learn to share and to get along with others.
"Johnny likes to play, too", she says to me. "I know you will play with him."

My mommy knows I need to be active—to move, to play, to run, to jump. She knows I learn through play. Sometimes she plays with me. Sometimes she lets me play alone.

My mommy helps me in my learning and in my growing up.

How Do I Provide Guidance For My Child?

I understand that my child is not a grown up

He is a child and I know he should act like one. He thinks as a child and that is different from the way I think. This helps me give guidance.

I show my child things

I show him what is safe and not safe; what he can touch, or squeeze, or throw. I show him how to do things—but not if it is too hard for him. Then he would become unhappy and give up. I show him how to keep trying . . . not to give up too easily while I help to make his task a success.

My child needs some freedom

He needs a little leeway to be himself. He needs to be able to look about and find things—spools to roll, string to tie, boxes to stack. He doesn't need me always to be warning—"Stay out of that" . . . "Quit that" . . . "Stop that" Not unless I have a good reason. If I do this I may make him shy and afraid to try.

Yes, my child needs guidance. Good guidance.

I encourage lots of play

I know that he learns many things through play. I talk to him as he plays to help him understand meanings of many words. I get out my plastic mixing bowls to stack, pots and pans to play with, old catalogs to cut and boxes to make a train!

While I am doing my work he plays alone. I want him to try out new things, to become curious, because he can learn many things by himself. I want him to play with others, too. He needs to learn that he can't always have his own way, that sometimes it is good to share, to take turns, to make friends.

INDEPENDENCE

My mommy lets me do things for myself.
I want to button my clothes and she lets me try.
When it is too hard for me, she helps me.
She thinks I can do many more things for myself.
I can tie my shoes and zip my zippers.
I know where to put up my things.
My mommy says I am growing up **BIG!**

What Am I Doing To Help My Child Develop Independence?

I let him try things

This isn't always easy because I have to clean up later. But I know that he can't learn to do things for himself unless I give him a chance. And sometimes I get out of patience waiting! I could do it so much faster and get it over with!

I give my child things to do

My child can help me fold clothes — the little things. He can pick up his own clothes and I can teach him where to put them. He can put away playthings — (and they don't have to be "bought"). He can help me with the garbage and other things like dusting and picking up in the yard. He can stir the cake or mix the juice. And there are forks and knives to be put on the table.

I teach my child about work

Sure it's fun when they are little. It isn't really work at all. But I feel my child should know what work is and when he is older he will have a better personal feeling about working. When my child hands his dad, or someone in the home, the nails they are using to do a repair job, I say "You are helping with the work". When I give him a small dust cloth while I use a large one, I call it "work".

I talk to him about other people's work. The policeman, the garbage collector, the doctor, the teacher, the fireman, the milkman — and all the people who help us. I want him to appreciate these people for the things they do.

I encourage

I encourage my child to finish a task that he has started. If he is having too much trouble and seems to be getting irritable, I will offer a helping hand . . . but it MUST BE FINISHED.

I encourage my child to follow simple directions which have a definite purpose. "Please close the door. It is getting cold in the room". "Bring me the potatoes to peel". I compliment my child for the work that he does — not so much "My what a smart boy," but rather . . . "You did a good job!" Then he will be proud of what he has accomplished!

RESPECT FOR OTHERS

My mommy knows I need to grow up to be good.
She is always telling me "You are a good helper".
I like that!
She knows I need to like others.
She wants me to be comfortable with them.
I don't know much about people.
But my mommy helps me learn.

How Do I Help Develop Respect For Others?

I talk
I talk about my concern for the child without a coat on a cold day and the little boy who has to walk on crutches.

I talk about the little old lady who has trouble walking up the steps alone and about the lonely old man next door, the child without a mother, the man without a home.

I don't over-do this. I give it in small doses.

I tell
I tell my child when he doesn't like someone... "but Johnny needs you. He needs you for his friend".
I tell my child, "Maybe Sammy hits because he has a problem". "Perhaps Sara cries because she feels lonely".

I want my child to understand people and their needs, and that they are different, look different and may act different. I compliment my child for helping others.

"I'm sure Mrs. Jones was proud to have you help rake the leaves". "It was thoughtful of you not to yell in the yard since Grandpa needed to get his nap".

I remind
I remind my child that it hurts Jimmy to be called "Fatso", or James to be called "Skinny Legs", or Freddy to be called "Runt".

I remind my child that it isn't kind to laugh at the mistakes of others or to make fun of them.

I read and explain and ask
Reading can make my child develop good thoughts and good feelings. I read stories, look at pictures, and ask questions to cause my child to think. Was Johnny nice to his friend? How would you have felt if this had happened to you? Wasn't it nice of Lisa to share? Why didn't "The Little Red Hen" share her bread?

Reading helps my child develop good traits. I want my child to grow up to be kind and considerate, dependable and honest, responsible and fair.

And if I begin at an early age to teach these traits, he will be likely to remember these when he is older.

THE BOWDOIN METHOD

CONFIDENCE

My mommy wants me to have good feelings about myself.
She wants me to believe that **I AM IMPORTANT!**
She helps me believe in myself.
She helps me believe **I CAN DO!**
She tells me I am **REALLY SPECIAL!**
I think she is really special, too!

How Can I Help My Child Develop Confidence?

My child needs something to be proud of.

It could be a painting or drawing that looks like nothing to me. But if he has tried and says "Look Mom" . . . I look! I encourage him to tell me about it and we will put it up in the house.

Or perhaps he has picked up the leaves that I have been raking and I say "My how nice the yard looks". He holds out his chest and has a twinkle in his eye!

He has done something that is giving him pleasure because I like it!

I can help him believe in himself.

Praise. Compliment. These are important when my child earns it. But if it is not earned, of course I would not lie. Perhaps I can give him something easy enough to do that he can do successfully. After all, I can't expect my baby to walk until he can sit alone.

And I wouldn't want my young child to be given a job that is far too hard for him to do. He would never feel pleased with himself if he feels too let down.

I can keep from comparing him with others

My child is an individual. There is just one like him. No more. I know there are many things which go into his make-up. And I want him to be **HIMSELF,** no other! I want him to compare himself with **HIMSELF!**

"But Mommy I can't climb as high as Johnny", says my child. And I reply "But there are other things you can do well".

This does not mean that my child will never have failure. Sometimes children learn from having a little failure. But too much of it can destroy his good feelings! And it does not mean that I should be satisfied with less than the best! But my pleasure will come when my child has done the best that **HE** can do with no comparison to what others do.

If I can help my child develop this feeling—this good, positive feeling of confidence, or self-worth, or whatever you want to call it. . . . I will have helped him **BELIEVE** in himself for what he is!

Then I would hope that he will grow up to be a solid citizen, a worthy family member, a person who **DOES** because he **THINKS HE CAN!**

My mother really likes me!
And do you know something!
I really like her, too!

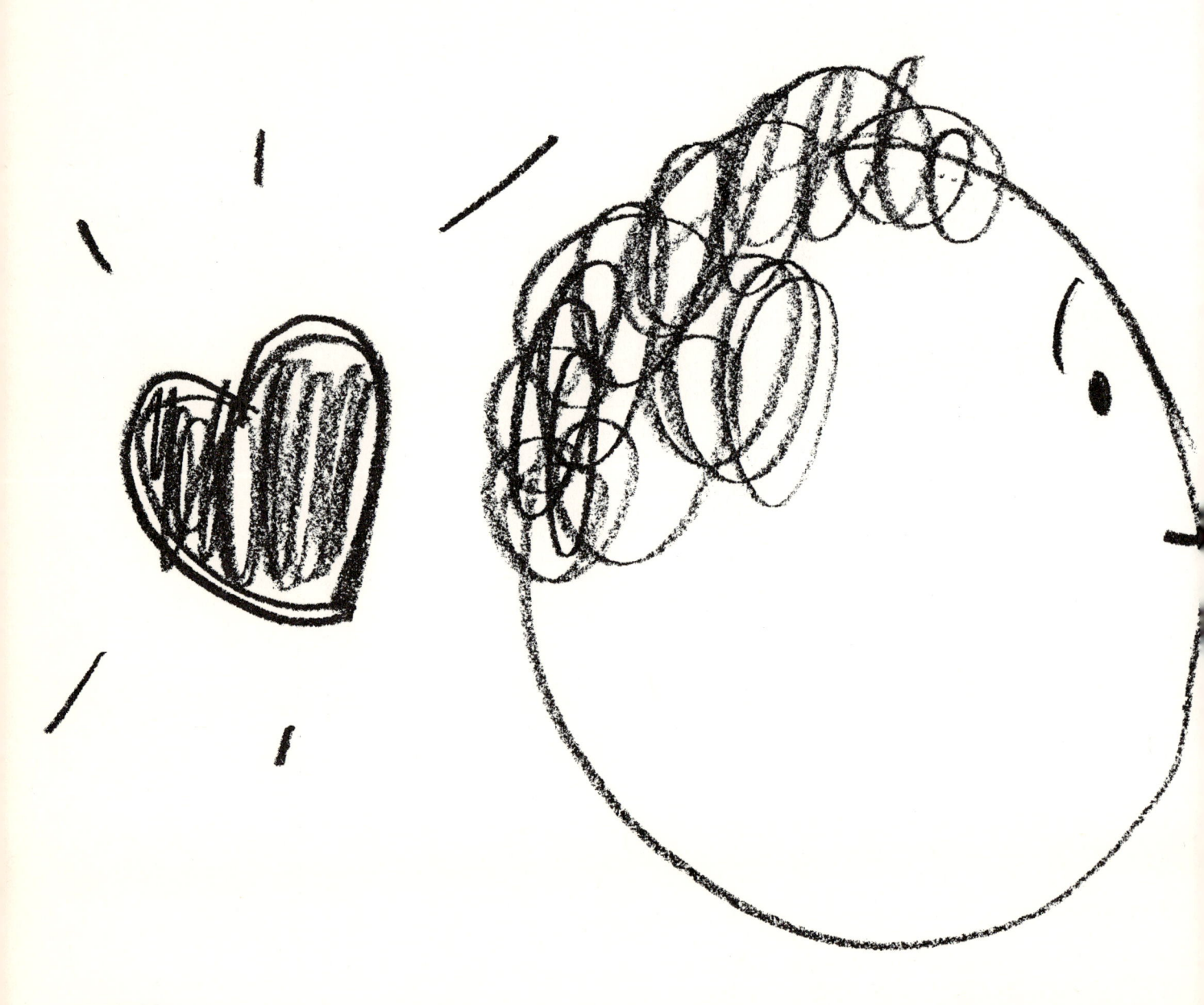

THE BOWDOIN METHOD

PAGE 135

NOTES

PARENT ACTIVITIES FOR
HOW TO HELP YOUR CHILD DEVELOP EMOTIONALLY

Activity One — Evaluating

Five parents are speaking to their child. Some are developing the basic need listed. One or two parents are <u>not</u>. Place an (X) beside these parents.

Independence
(   ) Parent: "Come, help me stir the cake."
(   ) Parent: "Put your socks in the bottom drawer."
(   ) Parent: "You can put on your own shirt."
(   ) Parent: "You are too little. You'll make a mess!"
(   ) Parent: "Look at Pete. He can dress himself!"

Respect for Others
(   ) Parent: "Wasn't it nice of John to share his candy!"
(   ) Parent: "It isn't kind to laugh at the mistakes of others."
(   ) Parent: "I know Mrs. Herndon was happy to have you help her."
(   ) Parent: "Paul isn't eating enough. Let's nickname him Runt."
(   ) Parent: "The garbage collector is our good helper."

Security
(   ) Parent: "Don't be afraid. I will be here."
(   ) Parent: "If you don't behave I may leave you."
(   ) Parent: "Of course it may hurt a little, but not for long."
(   ) Parent: "If you aren't nice daddy may leave us."

Guidance
(   ) Parent: "Stop that! Don't do that! Stay out of that!"
(   ) Parent: "Nell likes to play too. I know you will let her play with your doll."
(   ) Parent: "Go build a barn with the blocks. You can play all by yourself."
(   ) Parent: "Why don't you look around and find something to play with?"
(   ) Parent: "No, I'm sorry. I cannot let you throw blocks."

Control
(   ) Parent: "You may have bad feelings, but I can't let you hurt others."
(   ) Parent: "Do you have your self control, Herbie?"
(   ) Parent: "I want you to play quietly. The baby is asleep."
(   ) Parent: "Remember you can't do that. That is one of our rules."
(   ) Parent: "Quit that! I've told you three times already!"

Acceptance
(   ) Parent: "I like you just the way you are!"
(   ) Parent: "I wish you could be like David!"
(   ) Parent: "You are such a good helper."
(   ) Parent: "You are not happy but I love you."
(   ) Parent: "I know I can depend on you *every day*."

Confidence
(   ) Parent: "I know you can do this job!"
(   ) Parent: "You can't climb as high as Marvin."
(   ) Parent: "You are little, so I'll give you something easy."
(   ) Parent: "You are REALLY special to me!"
(   ) Parent: "Just wait until grandmother comes. She'll be so proud of you!"

Love
(   ) Parent: "Do you know I love you very much?"
(   ) Parent: "You are very important to me!"
(   ) Parent: "I love you but sometimes I don't like the way you act."
(   ) Parent: "Sometimes you make me wonder what I'll ever do with you!"
(   ) Parent: "How can I stand it any longer?"

THE BOWDOIN METHOD

Activity Two — Complete The Blanks
The first letter is given. Try to complete the sentence without using your book.

1. Giving "things" is not giving l_____.
2. To love is not to s_____.
3. Parents cannot let children do as they please but they can be f_____.
4. If parents overprotect children they will become too d_____ upon them.
5. The words "self c_____" are good words to teach your child.
6. To control children, parents need to be f_____ but never h_____.
7. Parents need to set limits on a child's behavior and stick to it e_____ d_____.
8. If your child does not have some freedom she/he may grow up to be s_____ and a_____.
9. Things seem to go better in a home in which parents keep their voices s_____ and p_____.
10. Eight basic needs which parents should give children to help them grow up to be emotionally healthy are:

    A_____ L_____
    C_____ L_____
    C_____ S_____
    G_____ R_____ for O_____

Activity Three — Circle "Yes" or "No"

Yes No 1. It gives children security to say, "But you MUST."
Yes No 2. Good parents shame children for bad behavior.
Yes No 3. If your child is secure she/he will be able to "turn you loose."
Yes No 4. Children should be allowed to cry at times.
Yes No 5. Sometimes a threat can be good even if you know you cannot carry it out.
Yes No 6. To be a good example parents should sometimes say "I am sorry."
Yes No 7. Children should be taught that sometimes it is all right to get angry as long as others are not hurt.
Yes No 8. Seldom should children be told WHY behavior is not acceptable.
Yes No 9. Sometimes children learn by having some failures.
Yes No 10. Comparing children with others can sometimes make them work harder and with more ease.

(Did you have 4 "No" answers?)

Activity Four — Read and Evaluate
Read the Child's pages. On each page ask yourself "Could my child say this?" Write "Yes", "No", or "Undecided."

Page 118_____   Page 126_____

Page 120_____   Page 128_____

Page 122_____   Page 130_____

Page 124_____   Page 132_____

Read the Parent pages. On each page ask yourself "Am I doing these things?" Write "Yes", "No", or "Some of Them".

Page 119 _____   Page 127 _____

Page 121 _____   Page 129 _____

Page 123 _____   Page 131 _____

Page 125 _____   Page 133 _____

Activity Five — My Personal Commitment

The early years are the formative years. Almost from birth your child becomes aware of you and begins to sense your feelings. If she/he consistently feels "My parents like me", if it shines through even when you are expressing disapproval... your child is on the way toward a healthy launching! Parents can't be perfect and should not feel guilty, but should make efforts in the right direction.

The following behaviors will help your child grow up emotionally strong and mentally healthy. Are you doing some of these? Check each under the appropriate column.

		I do this	I do not do this	I shall try
1.	I tell my child with words and actions that I love him/her			
2.	I touch my child when comfort is needed			
3.	I try my best to be pleasant, happy and smile a lot			
4.	I try to keep my voice soft and pleasant			
5.	I accept my child for being him/herself			
6.	I do not allow my child to do as she/he pleases			
7.	I never shame or frighten my child			
8.	I try not to overprotect my child			
9.	I don't threaten unless I mean to carry it out			
10.	I give my child as many new experiences as I can			
11.	I am teaching my child the words "self control"			
12.	I apologize to my child when I feel I have done wrong			
13.	I "set limits" and my child knows what she/he can or cannot do			
14.	I am firm but kind in trying to control my child			
15.	I say, "I know how you feel but you cannot do that"			
16.	I do not expect my child to have the behavior of a grown up			
17.	I encourage lots of play alone and with others			
18.	I give my child freedom to explore (a little leeway)			
19.	I allow my child to help even though I could do it much more quickly			
20.	I encourage my child to finish a task that she/he has started			
21.	I teach my child to understand others that are different or less fortunate			
22.	I help my child understand people who look different			
23.	When I read, I try to use the content of the story to build good traits (values)			
24.	I try to help my child believe in him/herself			
25.	I do not compare my child with other children			
26.	I try to give my child something to do that she/he can be proud of			
27.	I prepare my child when she/he has to face something new or strange			
28.	I teach my child that home is a good, safe place to be			
29.	I teach my child not to "make fun" of others			
30.	I try to teach my child to like him/herself and to like others			

NOTES

Chapter 5

HOW TO DEVELOP YOUR CHILD'S SELF ESTEEM

Dear Parent:

GOOD FEELINGS ARE IMPORTANT. Educators believe that our children learn better when they feel good about themselves.

It is well known that intelligence has a part in how easy your child finds learning. But, at the same time, many persons believe today that more than any other thing the feelings which your child has will affect his ability to learn.

Educators call this "The Self Concept." It really means whether or not the child has confidence in himself, whether or not he has a feeling of self worth and importance.

HOW YOUR CHILD FEELS MAY BE MORE IMPORTANT THAN WHAT HE KNOWS. This may be a shocking statement to you! But it is felt that most young people and adults who get into serious trouble have very poor feelings about themselves.

If your child does not have a good feeling about himself and others, learning will come harder for him. The feeling "I am nobody" will cause a child not to try as hard, not to want to learn, not to care whether he is successful. And this feeling may create learning problems or behavior problems.

The self-concept is a learned thing. It is taught in the home (and in the school) by the things you say, the way you look, the reactions you have, the things you do to your child and for him.

How can your child learn to think well of himself? What can you do?

That's what this chapter is all about.

Happy Teaching!

Ruth Bowdoin

Have A Happy Home

Nothing contributes more to your child's feeling good about himself than a happy home and a happy school.

Parents and teachers are strong influences in helping to develop this feeling.

Children need to feel that they live in a home or school in which they have some freedom, but in which they understand that there are rules for living.

And they need to have a part in making these rules. By doing so, they will have more respect for them and try more to live by them.

If a child knows that he will be treated fairly and with respect, he will be more at ease and comfortable.

"I Can Do It"

If your child's early years have been good ones, it will be hard for him to miss in the early years of school.

Your child must need to feel, "I can do that." If he has this feeling of belief in himself, he will be more likely to learn.

It is a strike against your child if he starts the early years in school with the thought that he is not good at things. When he begins to read, write, and spell, he needs to get a sense that he is somebody important.

But children have to be ready to learn the skills. Not all youngsters are ready for reading by the time they are six, for example. Children are different and don't learn at the same speed. If they are pushed or feel that the home or school is against them, they will have problems learning.

So set realistic goals for your child. Give him a chance to develop without pressures and without comparisons to others. If you do, he will have a good self-concept.

Help your child develop this good feeling by encouraging him when he feels he can't do something.

You may need to say, "Yes, you can. Come, I'll help you."

THE BOWDOIN METHOD

PAGE 143

"See this?"

When your child says this, what do you do?

Don't, for goodness sake, say, "Is that the best you can do?"

Don't say, "But a cow isn't purple."

And don't say, "Whoever heard of coloring one sock red and the other one green?"

You'll build up your child's feelings by making him proud of his accomplishments. And certainly [he] is proud enough of it to show it to you.

Better say, then, "Yes, that's very nice. Would you like to hang it in your room? But first may I show it to Grandma?"

Show Interest In Your Child's Work

Praise

A pat on the back.
A smile.
A cheerful and encouraging word now and then.

You can help develop good feelings within your child when you give him praise. But it's important that the praise be deserved. If you praise every little thing, he will know you're not being sincere.

This will keep them from trying.

It is very good to praise what they have done rather than praise them:

"My, how pretty your room looks."

"It's nice of you to help me with the baby."

"Mary, I liked the way you listened while Mrs. Jones was talking."

THE BOWDOIN METHOD

Make A Big "To-Do" Over Birthdays

Your child needs to feel good about himself to learn.

Make birthdays special. It doesn't take much time to make a simple cake and just a little money for a simple present.

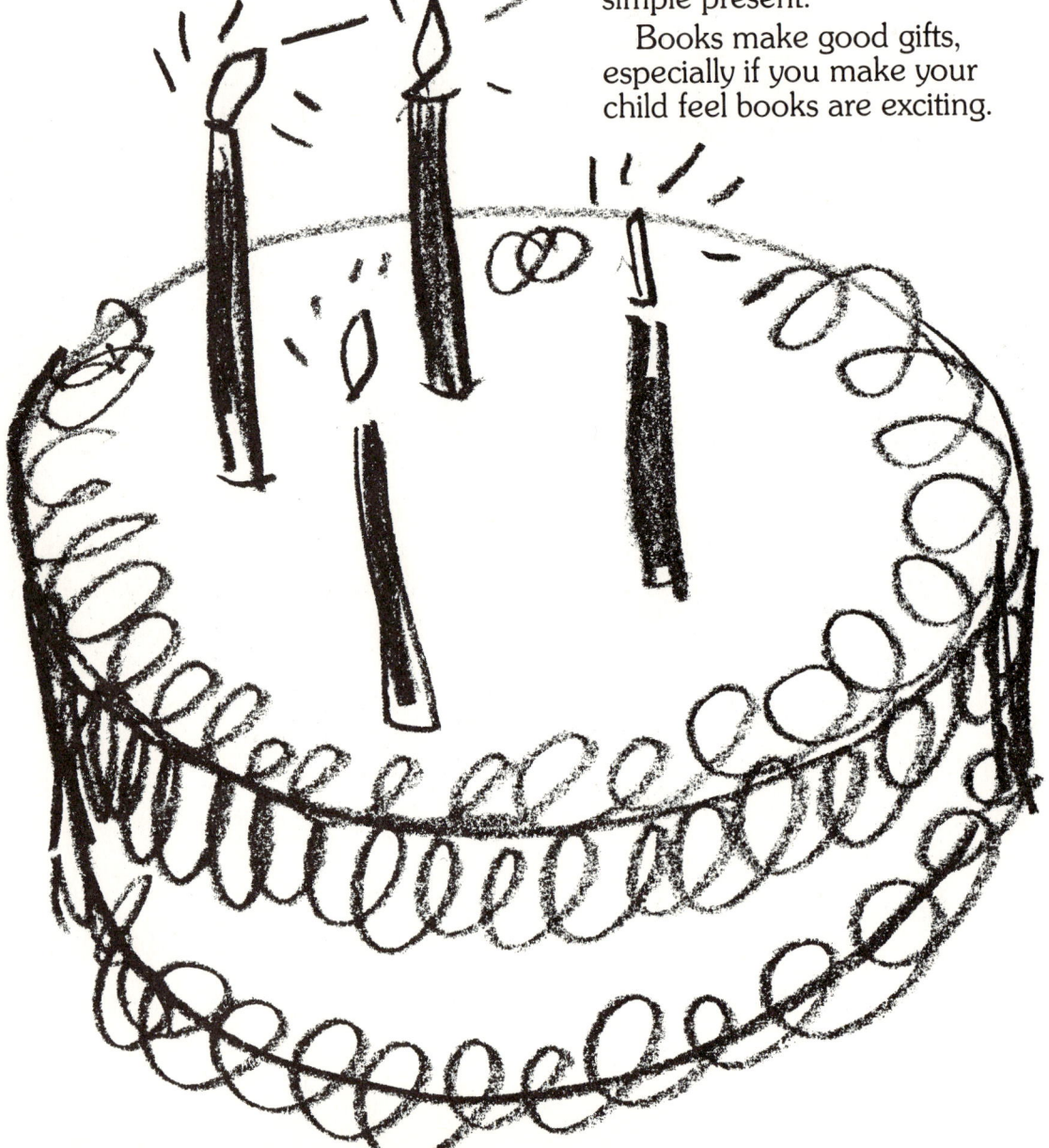

Books make good gifts, especially if you make your child feel books are exciting.

"I Can Do It Myself"

"Let me do it."

Most of the times it is much easier for us to do something than to let our children do it.

At different ages your child begins to want to do things. Let him. Give him as much responsibility as he can handle.

A child learns through working out his problems. He needs to make some choices. In this way he learns to do things which will make him proud of himself.

Let him try things. Interfere only when he is hurting others, when something is dangerous, or when something is destructive.

"I Can't Do It"

"I can't draw a horse. Make one for me."

Does your child ever say things like this? If he does, it's a fairly good sign that he does not feel competent about himself.

You may say, "Sure you can. Make it like *you* think it is. Draw it the way *you* like."

Then allow him to do it without saying, "That's not how to do it."

If you draw pictures for your child, he may feel that he has to do it as well as you do. But his eyes may not have developed to see things as you see them.

It is really only a scribble to you, but if it is his, he can have some pride, whether it looks right to you or not. This will help him develop a good feeling about himself. And he will feel that he *can* do things.

Look Into Your Child's Eyes

Of course it's impossible to stop every few minutes to listen to what your child has to say.

But a wise parent knows that listening can play a big part in making her child feel he is worthwhile.

Your child will know that you care when you stop long enough to look into his eyes as you listen to what he has to say.

This willingness to listen can help your child feel better about himself. When you listen, you are saying to him, "You are worthwhile." "You are important." "You *count*."

"Am I Better Than...?"

"Mommy, am I better than Dorothy?"

Children sometimes ask such questions.

The habit of "Am I better than...?" should be watched carefully. Each child should be given credit for what he is and what he can do without being compared to anyone else.

We probably should answer such questions by saying, "Why, I'm sure you must be better in some things than Dorothy. And Dorothy must be better in some things than you. I know I can't sew as well as her mother, but I am pretty good at driving."

Teach Your Child To Be Helpful

Perhaps your child is too young to do some things. But he can be taught to pick up clothes and toys.

Set aside one of the drawers near the bottom of your dresser especially for your young child. Teach the youngster to get his own things: "Go get your red socks to match your sweater."

Older children can be expected to be helpful with chores around the house — making beds, dusting, and folding clothes.

It's all good training.

If your child feels useful in the family, he will be much more likely to feel good about himself.

Try it and see.

Teach Your Child To Like Others

People look different from each other. They may have red hair and freckles, or black skin, or legs too long for their size. They may be fat or skinny or short or tall.

Teach your child, by your own good example, to enjoy and respect the differences in people.

If he learns this early, he will also be learning to believe in and appreciate himself.

When we lose patience, it's very easy for us to say this.

But when we do, our children feel that we think they *can't* learn.

They feel that we think they aren't very smart. And that hurts.

Then they may just give up and quit trying.

Have patience. Count to 10—or to 100 if you need to. Your child will profit.

"Can't You Learn Anything?"

"I Can't Be Perfect"

We can't expect children to be little adults.

If they are to feel confident and secure, they must be allowed times when things won't go the way we want them to.

It helps, too, if we admit to the mistakes we make. They need to know that we aren't perfect, either.

"I'm sorry. I shouldn't have yelled at you. I've been feeling bad all day."

Success Breeds Success

When children succeed—and we've talked about ways of helping them to—they begin to believe in their own abilities. And the more they believe they can do, usually the more they can do.

We need to teach our children that they can do some things well and that they may have problems with others. We expect of them the best they can do.

"I Like Me!"

You are, indeed, a lucky parent if your child can say "I like me."

Because if your child really feels this, he will be much more likely to find learning easier in school.

We want your child to feel:

"I can do things."
"I am important."
"I can learn."

You can have a very important part in these feelings by praising him for things he tries to do: complimenting him for things he does well; giving him things to do that are within his age level; making him feel that he is an important person in his own right; and by helping him know that his family loves and respects him.

Experiences

"I've seen that!" "I've done that!" And the child feels good. He feels good because he is able to identify with something he hears from a person or sees in a book.

He can understand what the words say because he has EXPERIENCED them. Experiences in doing and seeing things; experiences in going places—places in your own neighborhood; experiences in meeting new people and being made comfortable with them—all contribute to the child's learning.

The more he sees, hears, and does, the more he will know. The more he knows, the happier he is. The happier he is, the more easily he will learn. The more able he is to learn, the higher he regards himself. And so it goes . . !

"Stupid!"

Without thinking, some parents may have said this with their voice or face or eyes. Anything that makes a child feel 'no good'; anything that makes a child feel dumb; anything that makes a child feel that he is NOBODY will make him care little for himself.

When he cares little for himself, he will act in a way that shows it. It's just that simple. It's the cause of many of the child's learning and behavior problems. He acts this way because he feels it is expected of him.

"Everybody thinks I'm bad. So I might as well BE bad!" "She thinks I'm stupid. So I really can't learn!" A wise parent will guide older children not to call the little ones "stupid." Wise parents watch their language, also. They avoid other words that "belittle." Words like *dumb*, *lazy*, *dirty*, *mean*, *bad crazy*, *hateful*, *crybaby*, or *tattletale*. These hurt and hurts "add up" to bad things that happen inside your child.

Guilt Feelings

If your child is made to feel guilty, he feels sick inside. If he is made to feel guilty because of a mistake that he has made, he will not feel good about himself.

We teach that it is "right" to do some things; "wrong" to do others. If we "over-do" the guilt feelings, we make the child's acceptance of himself ever so much more difficult.

No misunderstanding! Of course, we can't allow children to feel that they can do wrong things. They must be corrected or given guidance. They may need punishment.

But a long string of "You ought to be ashamed our yourself!" will finally make the child feel that he is bad, unworthy, or unlovable. Whatever "digs" at the self over and over and over makes for bad feelings.

As parents, we allow for mistakes. That's the human thing to do. Correcting the mistakes is what counts.

"I'm Learning..."

Children need to feel that they are learning. "Watch me. I can do it!" "I can put a puzzle together." "I like to hear stories!" Your child needs to feel proud, important, and big!

Children differ from one another, and within themselves, as to what they can do. What is done depends upon the age and development at the time. When the time is right, success is good; or it could be failure and then success. Too many failures will keep the child feeling "small" and feeling "small" is bad for the self concept.

Start with the simple things. When these are learned, make the tasks a little harder. Encourage your child every step of the way. Keep building on what the child knows.

A wise parent does this without "pushing"! Too much stress can be harmful.

A good parent will help the child feel big!

"I'm Strong!"

"I can hop on one foot!" "I can drive a nail!" "I can run fast and climb a ladder!"

A child has a feeling of pride and a feeling of achievement about his physical growth. Motor skills are important. Young children need to develop their motor control.

With very little effort, parents may provide for this. Things may be found around the house or free at your market. Old pans, paper bags, sponges, plastic bottles, cardboard rolls, shoeboxes, cigar boxes, and cereal boxes all have a place in helping the child build things, hold things, and imagine things.

Father may make an old tire into a wonderful swing; or he may provide a plank for walking, boxes or barrels for crawling through, a big ball to catch.

The child may develop small muscles by cutting with blunt scissors. He may model with clay, play with puzzle parts, color, stack blocks, or pick up things to put in the parts of an egg carton. All are good for developing small muscles.

When your child feels "I am strong" he will begin to feel important! Father, Mother help him!

By about three a child begins to feel that he is really somebody! He is beginning to enjoy playing with other children. Earlier he chose to play alone. As he begins to get interested in playing with others, he may need help in making friends.

Most young children don't want to share and they hit, scratch, and fight! A wise parent steps in firmly and kindly.

"John wants to play with the truck now."
"You may have a turn at the swing after Mary."
"Sammy will share the blocks when he finishes his building."

Speak as if there is NO DOUBT. You may wonder if it will work, but the child will slowly learn what sharing is by getting help from a parent.

"Wasn't it fun to play with Susan today?"
"I really liked the way you played together."
"You are such good friends."

Talking to your child about friends will help him learn about them. When he is in primary grades, he will have fewer problems if he feels accepted by some of his classmates. As your child gets older, this becomes more and more important. Invite children to play in your home or yard. Provide the opportunity for friendships to grow.

"Others Like Me!"

How Do You Measure Your Child's Feelings?

Your child's best guesses about himself tell the story. How does your child feel?

(CIRCLE **YES** OR **NO**)

YES	NO	I can do many things.
YES	NO	I think I am getting better.
YES	NO	My father (mother) likes me.
YES	NO	I like my playmates. (If I am over three.)
YES	NO	My playmates like me.
YES	NO	I am strong.
YES	NO	I usually like to try.
YES	NO	I am encouraged to correct my mistakes.
YES	NO	I can't do all things well.

YES	NO	I know lots of things.
YES	NO	I can learn.
YES	NO	My parents will listen.
YES	NO	Nobody expects too much of me.
YES	NO	I don't fail often.
YES	NO	I like to do new things and meet new people.
YES	NO	Others seldom make me ashamed.
YES	NO	I sometimes get my way.
YES	NO	I often get my say.
YES	NO	I am a good helper.
YES	NO	I think I am getting better.

If your answer is "Yes" to most statements, your child has good feelings about himself. These feelings are important!

Help Your Child With His "Halo"

He isn't better than others. He isn't less important either. As a person, he is of equal worth. Teach your child that his worth does not depend upon:

    the color of his skin
    the kind of clothes he wears
    the money his family has
    the kind of work his father (or mother) does
    the kind of house he lives in

If you as a parent feel this way, your child will feel this way too. Feelings are "caught" as well as "taught." This is the secret to a good start in life. It will help your child to "face-up" now. It will also help him "face-up" later. Pride, not overdone, is necessary for good feelings.

PARENT ACTIVITIES FOR
HOW TO DEVELOP YOUR CHILD'S SELF-ESTEEM

These are ways of developing a good self concept. Complete the blanks:

1. A wise parent knows that l _ _ _ _ _ _ _ _ to him can make the child feel worthwhile.
2. Praise will develop good feelings but it should be d _ _ _ _ _ _ _.
3. The parent may build good feelings by making children proud of their
   a _ _ _ _ _ _ _ _ _ _ _ _ _ _
4. Give your child a chance to develop without p _ _ _ _ _ _ _ and without
   c _ _ _ _ _ _ _ _ _ _ _ to others.
5. If your children are treated f _ _ _ _ _ _ and with r _ _ _ _ _ _ _ they will be more at ease and comfortable.
6. Teach your child to enjoy and respect the d _ _ _ _ _ _ _ _ _ _ _ in p _ _ _ _ _ _.
7. We can't expect children to be l _ _ _ _ _ a _ _ _ _ _ _.
8. Give your children as much r _ _ _ _ _ _ _ _ _ _ _ _ as they can handle.
9. If your children feel u _ _ _ _ _ in the family, they will be much more likely to feel good about themselves.
10. Provide the opportunity for f _ _ _ _ _ _ _ _ _ _ to grow.

(Answers pages 149, 145, 144, 143, 142, 152, 154, 147, 151, 162 in this sequence)

Review your book and underline the following:

When you listen to your child you are saying three things. Underline these on page 149.

On page 156 underline five things you can do to make your child feel "I like me!"

Developing the child's physical body gives your child a feeling of achievement. Underline at least ten things which will develop the large and small muscles. (page 161)

On page 164 underline five things you teach your child that his/her worth does <u>NOT</u> depend upon.

The following are situations in the home which make the child feel unworthy. Read each one and check the things which the parent should have done. (You will have more than one check.) (Ellen is getting dressed for school.)

Ellen: I want to get my own socks!

Mother: You can't find yellow ones. Besides, the drawer is too high. I'll do it myself.

Mother should:

_____ Put the socks in a lower drawer.

_____ Show Ellen the yellow blouse and tell her to find the socks that match.

_____ Explain that she is too little to do this.

_____ Praise Ellen for wanting to get her socks.

* * * * * * * * *

THE BOWDOIN METHOD

(Father is raking leaves while Eric looks on)

Eric: Let me help. I want to help.

Father: You can't help! The rake is too big. Besides, I'm in a hurry. You're in my way!

Father should:

_____ Thank Eric for wanting to help.

_____ Tell him he can help pick the leaves up when he gets them in a pile.

_____ Let him try to rake if Father has another rake.

_____ Send Eric off to play in the swing.

* * * * * * * * *

(Father is building a house for the dog. David is wanting to help but father knows it is too difficult for David to handle.)

David: Let me help.

Father: No. This is too hard and you're in my way!

Father should:

_____ Talk enthusiastically about what he is doing.

_____ Ask David to hold the piece of lumber while he nails.

_____ Give David a play hammer and a scrap piece of wood and let him play beside him.

_____ Send David inside.

* * * * * * * * *

(Mother is busy in the kitchen.)

Carolyn: Mamma, I want some juice.

Mother: Sit here at the table and you may have some.

(Mother pours the juice and gives it to Carolyn who promptly spills it on her clean blouse.)

Mother: Now look at you! You have juice all over you! You are so messy! And you cause me so much trouble when I need to be cooking dinner!

Mother should say:

_____ "I believe you have had an accident, but you can help me clean it up." *(gives her a sponge)*

_____ "Why are you so clumsy? Must I always watch you. You're no baby!"

_____ "Don't fret. We will make it clean. That's what clothes washers are for."

_____ "If you'd sit still this wouldn't have happened. Sometimes I wonder about you Carolyn... whether you're smart!"

* * * * * * * * *

Rate each of the following responses to a situation. Use <u>GOOD</u>, <u>FAIR</u> or <u>POOR</u> in the blank provided.

Naomi shows her Father a picture which she has just made for him. She is obviously very proud of it! How do you rate the following three responses?

_____ "The picture is good but I don't know what it is."

_____ "What in the world is it?"

_____ "Tell me about your picture."

* * * * * * * * *

William, age 5, is playing "catch" with his Father. Father gets disgusted with his ineptness and tells him that his brother Sam could do that well at age 4. Rate these responses.

_____ "You are just not going to be able to run fast enough."

_____ "We need to practice more."

_____ "You may have trouble catching but you sure are sharp at pitching!"

* * * * * * * * *

Four-year old Ian comes into the house screaming as if he were in severe pain, crying "My finger — I broke my finger!". Rate the responses of the parent.

_____ "Heavenly days! I thought you were half-killed. You know that doesn't hurt!"

_____ "Of course it hurts honey. Try not to cry!"

_____ "I know it hurts. Come and I'll make it well. Let me rub it and kiss it. That will make the hurting stop!"

* * * * * * * * *

Gary, a six-year old, wanted another piece of candy. It was almost time for dinner. Rate the responses of the parent.

_____ "One piece is enough for now because we will be having dinner soon. After you eat your vegetables you may have another piece if you're still hungry."

_____ "You've already had one piece and you act like a greedy pig. This is the third time time you've asked! You heard me the first time! I'm boss around here!"

_____ "Absolutely not. Too much candy is not good for you."

* * * * * * * * *

Six-year old Kenneth was reading to his mother from his primer. He came across a word (where) that he didn't know. Rate mother's response.

_____ "Think. You are not thinking, Kenneth. What word would make sense? You know that."

_____ "I've told you that word over and over and OVER and still you don't know!"

_____ "The word is "where." That's not an easy word. Mother will remember to write it down with the other words that begin like it and we will work on these . . . what, when, where. You'll soon learn them."

THE BOWDOIN METHOD

The following is a list of words which you may use in different situations to help your child have good feelings. Read each one and <u>place an X</u> beside those which you are not presently using but you would like to remember to use when the occasion presents itself.

___ "What a good helper you are!"	___ "Oh, I like that!"
___ "I like the way you tried!"	___ "That's so good!"
___ "You are really improving!"	___ "Wonderful!"
___ "That's very sweet of you!"	___ "You are certainly a good thinker!"
___ "I knew I could trust you!"	___ "That's pretty. Let's put it up in your room."
___ "You really do have your self-control."	___ "I like the way you finished the job."
___ "Thank you for helping me!"	___ "Congratulations!"

* * * * * * * * * *

Read the following "Role Play." List several things that are <u>good</u> and several things that are <u>wrong</u> with the parent's behavior.

Parent: Come in here!! I want you to look at the book with me.

Child: No . . . I'm playing!

Parent: Playing my eye! I said come here and I don't mean maybe! *(child comes in sniffing a little)*

Parent: Now where did I put that book? *(Looks, mumbles under breath — finds it.)* Now sit here close to me.

Child: *(obviously wanting the parent's approval)* You love me, Mamma?

Parent: Yes, of course I do! But sometimes I don't like the way you act!

Child: Pretty book!

Parent: Wait. Don't start looking at the pictures! I've got to get my glasses!

Child: Now weed to me!

Parent: You don't say "weed" . . . say "read." You talk like a baby!

Child: I ain't no baby, am I?

Parent: Of course not. Mother is sorry I spoke harshly. I guess I'm just tired.

Child: *(tries to hold book)* Look, I see chicks!

Parent: Let me hold the book. You just look! Yes, I see some pretty yellow chicks. Could we count them?

Child: One, three, four!

Parent: One, TWO, three, four! Count with me. *(child counts correctly this time).*

Parent: Good thinking! Which chick is different . . . not like the others?

(Parent reads several pages enthusiastically. When the child starts wiggling parent ends the session pleasantly.)

What GOOD things did you observe?	What WRONG things
_____	_____
_____	_____
_____	_____
_____	_____
_____	_____

Chapter 6

HOW TO CONTROL YOUR CHILD WITH GOOD WORDS

Dear Parent:

Words talk. They say so many things. They make children **happy** or they make them **sad**.

There are happy words and sad ones! They make children feel that they are Somebody . . . that they are important . . . or that they are Nobody and are not loved!

The words you use can make your child FEEL GOOD INSIDE. They help you CONTROL WITHOUT BAD FEELINGS. This is very important to your child's learning.

Practice using the words on the "Do" side. You will be happier. Your child will respond better.

Happy Teaching!

Ruth Bowdoin

DON'T SAY...

"You're NO GOOD!"

**This is destructive.
Many times a child will misbehave if we think that he will!**

DO SAY...

"What a fine boy (or girl) you are!"

If we can believe this, a child will usually live up to our expectations.

DON'T SAY...

"I can NEVER depend on you!"

If your child believes this, he will never be dependable.

PAGE 172

THE BOWDOIN METHOD

DO SAY...

"I want you to be a good helper. Most times you are!"

This is encouraging.

THE BOWDOIN METHOD

PAGE 173

DON'T SAY...

"SHUT UP!"

A loud, rasping voice
only adds to tension and an unhappy home life.

DO SAY...

"Steady, John." "Quiet, Mary."

"Are you using your inside voice?"

When a child needs correcting, often a question as a reminder may be all you will need.

DON'T SAY...

"Aren't you ASHAMED of yourself?"

Guilt is not good.

DO SAY...

"Mother is disappointed.
I depend on you to do better.
If it happens again,
I will have to punish you!"

Speak quietly and calmly.

THE BOWDOIN METHOD

DON'T SAY...

"You hear me! I said, 'Behave,' and I don't mean maybe! I'll tell your daddy tonight!"

This creates an unhappy home life.

PAGE 178 THE BOWDOIN METHOD

DO SAY...

"Do you have your self-control?"
Or...
"Are you being a good helper?"

Simply asking the question may do the work for you.

THE BOWDOIN METHOD

DON'T SAY...

"I don't like you when you are bad!"

Your child needs to feel loved although you do not approve of his behavior.

THE BOWDOIN METHOD

DO SAY...

"I love you..., but I do not like the way you act!"

Be kind ... but very firm!

DON'T SAY...

"I've told you OVER and OVER... and still you don't know!"

This makes a child feel that something is wrong with him, that he *can't* learn!

PAGE 182

THE BOWDOIN METHOD

DO SAY...

"This is not easy to learn!
We will work on it at another time!
I will help you!"

**Patience is needed.
Learning may be slow. It takes much repetition.**

DON'T SAY...

"I'll whip you! This is three times I've told you to stop!"

A threat not carried out is not the answer.

DO SAY...

"I'm sorry, you CAN NOT do that because...."

Carry out the first time, firmly, consistently, kindly. Tell children *why*, then punish if you need to do so.

DON'T SAY...

"Why in the world can't you learn? Red is the ONLY color you know!"

This destroys feelings of success.

DO SAY...

"I'm glad you have learned your red color. How smart you are!"

A child thrives on a well deserved compliment.

THE BOWDOIN METHOD

DON'T SAY...

"I mean it! I said give her some of your candy!"

This creates bad feelings.

PAGE 188

THE BOWDOIN METHOD

DO SAY...

"Jane likes candy, too!
How nice to share with her!"

**Speak as if you are sure your child will do it without being forced.
See if it works.**

THE BOWDOIN METHOD

DON'T SAY...

"You hear me?
I said listen!"

If we use threatening loud voices, children will tune us out.
They get so they don't care what we say!

DO SAY...

"My, what sharp ears you have!"

Approve, compliment, praise!

THE BOWDOIN METHOD

DON'T SAY...

"You are a CRYBABY!
You KNOW you are not hurt."

Of course, he may be!
Why say he isn't?

THE BOWDOIN METHOD

DO SAY...

"Come, I'll kiss it well."
Or...
"Let me hold you until it stops hurting!"

Usually the child will stop right away if the hurt is a little one!

DON'T SAY...

"Just LOOK at you! I SAID GET UP THAT MESS!"

Of course, he should clean it up.

PAGE 194 — THE BOWDOIN METHOD

DO SAY...

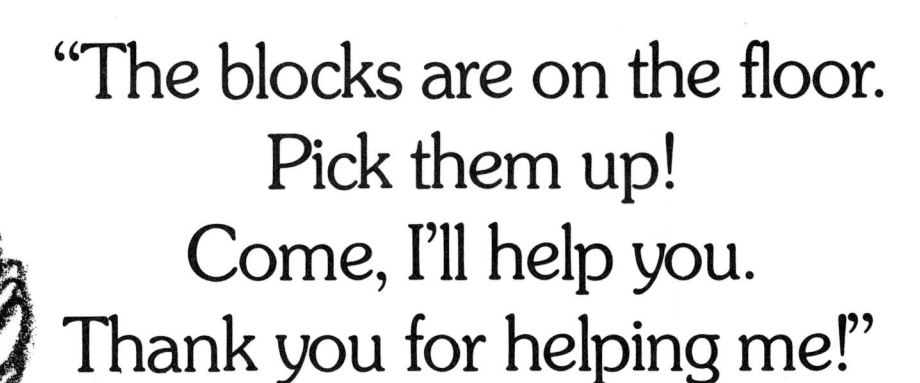

"The blocks are on the floor.
Pick them up!
Come, I'll help you.
Thank you for helping me!"

**The attitude is better.
Attitudes are important.**

DON'T SAY...

"I don't think you can do it! You are too clumsy!"

This destroys a child's desire to try.

DO SAY...

"Try hard! I think you can do it!"
Later...
"I knew you could do it!"

**If they "think they can,"
they usually *can* do it if it is reasonable.**

THE BOWDOIN METHOD

DON'T SAY...

"Wash that face!
Straighten that skirt!

Pull up those pants!
Quit sucking that thumb!"

Continual nagging destroys a child's good feelings.

DO SAY...

"How pretty you will look when you get all cleaned up!"

A child needs the incentive, the praise, in order to *want* to do.

THE BOWDOIN METHOD

PAGE 199

DON'T SAY...

"I tell you.... I'm sick and tired of the way you are acting!"

Yes you are! But nagging is not the answer.

THE BOWDOIN METHOD

DO SAY...

"You know it's a good thing that I love you so much!"

You are out of patience! Continual nagging makes things worse. If the misdeed is bad enough for punishment, do so kindly, consistently, and firmly.

PARENT ACTIVITIES FOR
HOW TO CONTROL YOUR CHILD WITH GOOD WORDS

Activity One — Evaluating Expressions

Evaluate responses to a situation with children. Use "Good," "Fair," "Poor."

Bruce, age 6, has been asked by his mother to take a small bag of garbage to a container. On the way he accidentally spills it.

_____ I can NEVER depend on you.

_____ I'm not happy about this!

_____ Clean this up. I need you to be my good helper!

* * * * *

Helen and Larry, age 5, are playing in the house. The baby is sleeping and mother is anxious.

_____ Use your "inside voice." The baby is sleeping.

_____ SHUT UP!

_____ Be quieter! I've told you twice!

* * * * *

Jose, age 6, tells his father that he is afraid to play with Hal because he fights.

_____ Aren't you ashamed to be afraid?

_____ I can understand how you feel. Find another playmate.

_____ Maybe he won't do it again.

* * * * *

Sally, age 5, shoved Ruthie into a swing and hurt her.

_____ You are too big to do a thing like that!

_____ I'm sorry, but I can't let you hurt Ruthie.

_____ You hear me! I'll tell your daddy tonight!

Lance and Gary, age 4, were playing with toys. Lance picked up a toy and threw it at Gary.

_____ You are acting ugly. What in the world is wrong?

_____ I don't like you when you're bad.

_____ You can NOT do that. I love you but not the way you act!

* * * * *

Father was helping Jose learn to count to twenty. Jose had difficulty.

_____ I've told you these over and OVER and still you don't know!

_____ I'll help you. You can learn it.

_____ We went over this yesterday. Try hard this time.

* * * * *

Mother told Lucy, a four-year old, to share the candy with Susie. Lucy promptly refused. "My candy!", she said.

_____ I said give Susie some candy. I mean it! You heard me!

_____ We learn to share. If you don't I'll put it away.

_____ Susie likes candy too. I know you'll share with her.

* * * * *

Daddy was saying something important to six-year old Herman who obviously was not listening.

_____ Herman, put on your sharp ears!

_____ I said listen! You heard me!

_____ Six-year old boys listen!

PAGE 202 THE BOWDOIN METHOD

Activity Two — Selecting Expressions

Place an (X) before the expressions which generally contribute to an unhappy home life with young children.

( ) You heard me!
( ) I'll tell your daddy.
( ) I don't mean maybe!
( ) I am ashamed of you!
( ) Just look at you! I'm sick and tired of this!
( ) I said STOP it!
( ) Mother is disappointed. You can do better.
( ) I don't like you when you're bad!
( ) This is three times I've told you to stop!
( ) I'm sorry. You can't do that. It hurts.
( ) Shut your mouth!
( ) I can't ever depend on you!

(Did you check all except two of the above?)

Place an (X) before the expressions which generally are effective with young children. These are "words that win children" and make for a more harmonious home life.

( ) Do you have your self control?
( ) What sharp ears you have!
( ) Steady, Julie!
( ) What a nice helper you are!
( ) Don't be a crybaby!
( ) Can't you learn?
( ) Are you using your "inside" voices?
( ) Quit sucking that thumb!
( ) I like the way you acted.
( ) You know you are not hurt!
( ) I told you that three times!
( ) Thank you for being so nice.

(Did you find seven good expressions?)

Activity Three — Making Judgments

Read each statement. Write "agree" or "disagree."

_____Using a threatening, loud voice is not good for the atmosphere in the home.

_____Speak as if you are sure your child will do what you ask.

_____A child thrives on a well deserved compliment.

_____It is best never to punish your child for bad behavior.

_____When your child understands, it is best to tell him/her WHY she/he can or cannot do a certain thing.

_____A threat not carried out can damage your relationship.

_____Be consistent, firm and kind if you want control of your child's behavior.

_____When there is bad behavior, your child needs to know she/he is not loved.

_____Parents need to use "good words" because these will help control your child without creating bad feelings.

(Did you find two statements with which you disagree?)

Activity Four — Evaluating A Dialogue

Read the dialogue and underline all statements that contribute to bad feelings and a home without harmony.

(Mother is watching television and she is in for a bad day! Gary is three years old. Apparently mother is not aware that with three-year-olds "No" is more popular than "Yes." Everything seems to go wrong.)

Mother: You heard me! I said STOP that noise!
(child does not listen)

Mother: Stop RIGHT NOW! I don't mean MAYBE!

Gary: No!

Mother: Are you saying "No" to ME? I'll whip you boy!
(Mother walks over and handles Gary roughly.)

Gary: *(crying)* You hurted me! You hurted me!

Mother: That's good enough for you. I don't love you when you're bad.

Gary: I not bad!

Mother: Oh, yes you are! I'm ashamed of you!

Gary: *(snuggling up beside mother)* Hold me.

Mother: No. I'm busy. You're too big to hold. Please be a good helper.
(Gary sucks thumb.)

Mother: Here you go! Get that thumb out of your mouth!
(Gary begins to whimper.)

Mother: Stop that crying! You're a crybaby!

Gary: I not a crybaby!

Mother: You're disputing me again! I can never depend on you when my program is on!

Activity Five — Reviewing The Book

List the number of the page or pages on which you find the "best" words to use for the situation.

Page _____ The child is making too much noise

Page _____ The child will not share

Page _____ The child cries because she/he says it hurts

Page _____ The child has trouble learning

Page _____ The child has not picked up toys

Page _____ The child has trouble listening

Page _____, _____, _____, _____ The child has been misbehaving

* * * * * * * * *

Complete the blanks.

1. A child will usually live up to our e_____.

2. A l_____ r_____ voice only creates tension.

3. When a child needs correcting often a q_____ as a reminder is all you need.

4. Your child needs to feel l_____ although you do not approve of his/her behavior.

5. Continual n_____ destroys the child's good feelings.

6. A child needs the i_____, the p_____ in order to WANT to do.

7. If the misdeed is bad enough for punishment, do so k_____, c_____ and f_____.

(Review pages 171, 174, 175, 180, 198, 199, 201 for answers.)

Chapter 7
HOW TO MANAGE YOUR CHILD FOR GOOD BEHAVIOR

Dear Parent:

Being a parent is hard business! It is so hard to know just what to do and say at just the right time. There are so many problems today and so many worries which you have as parents!

There just doesn't seem to be a simple way of being a parent. Not all things work with children. Nothing seems to work with some, especially when we are tired and get out of patience. You do not expect to be a perfect parent — no one is.

Some people will tell us one thing about managing children for desirable behavior; others tell us differently. It is hard to know just what to do. Personality conflicts are sure to arise and these will pass. But if a child lives in a home in which there is lots of fussing and bickering and where the home is not a happy one, it will show up in the behavior of the child.

All behavior has a cause. And sometimes WE cause it! This book contains suggestions which should keep problems from developing. I hope that you may use some of them.

Happy Teaching!

Ruth Bowdoin

Fuss, Fuss, Nag, Nag!

"Does my child need discipline?" parents ask.

Yes. But fussing and nagging will not get the job done.

There are ways to handle bad behavior. And most educators agree that children actually **want** discipline. Children feel insecure where there is no control.

A middle-of-the-road approach is usually best—that is, a balance between being too hard on a child and being too easy. A child can build up feelings of hatred, resentment, and rebellion—so he needs help to control his impulses. He needs help to learn self-control.

The following principles should be used in managing your child's behavior:

1. Be **consistent** in what you expect your child to do or not do.

2. Help your child to understand the **limits** set up.

3. **Praise** him when he deserves it.

4. Don't nag. **Be kind, but firm.**

5. Give your child **love,** but let him understand that to love him is not to let him do as he pleases.

Too Little Or Too Much?

Too little or too much discipline in the home may cause your child to have problems in school.

No two children are alike. And you're not like any other parent. But some things will work with most children. Try these:

1. Firmness **with kindness** will discipline your child, but the way you do it is important. Angry words may build bitterness in your child. Firmness can mean love and can build respect.

2. Be a good example. A child learns from the actions and attitudes he sees. Relax with your child.

3. No matter what age your child is, he wants you to tell him what he **can** and **can't** do. But explain why.

4. When you correct your child for bad behavior, say, "You are a good boy, but you cannot do that." Don't say, "You're a bad boy to do that."

5. Build up your child. Make him know that you are proud of him and love him.

Some Days "Yes," Some Days "No"

"I don't know what I can do. Some days Mom says, 'Yes,' and some days 'No.'"

This makes your child feel insecure. You have the authority to have him **do** or **not do** something. But do you use your authority the **same every day?** If you feel good and things are going well, do you let your child "get by" with almost anything? And on other days is almost everything off limits?

This gets troublesome for children. Sometimes Mom and Dad will let them do certain things. Sometimes they won't. The child just does not know how to behave or what to expect.

Psychologists have experimented with rats. They found that if rats get food some days by going through certain doors and other days they don't, the rats will become confused and act strange.

They believe the same happens to children **when we are not consistent.** Children do not get a chance to learn the proper behavior when we act this way.

Teach Politeness

Children do not just happen to be polite. They are taught by you in the home and by teachers in the school.

First of all, they learn by good examples. If we say polite words, they will. If we hold our tongues when we get angry, they will learn to.

If your child is taught politeness, he will make friends more easily. And if your child has friends, he will be happier and feel accepted and liked.

Some polite words:

"Excuse me" "Please" "Thank you" "You're welcome" "That's very good" "Come to see me" "I'm sorry" "Let me help you" "I like you" "You're invited to play with me."

Your youngsters will use these words only if you teach them.

"Mom, I Need Help To Control Myself"

All of us get angry sometimes. We should not be ashamed of this. But the young child often has trouble controlling anger. Sometimes he may even have a tantrum.

What do you do? Try different things. Sometimes it's best just to stand by and say nothing. Or he may be removed to another room. If he gets what he wants, he will know he can "handle" you. No one way will end all tantrums.

At the same time, a parent should know when the child is sleepy or tired. Also it helps if we remember that other parents' children act this way too.

After the tantrum is over, it is usually good to say, "I know how you must feel. I like to do things or have things that I can't. But work hard on your **self-control**." (You can use this word. Your child will soon know what it means.)

The Loving Hand

Look at your hand.
Is it a loving hand?
Or is it a "whip-hand"?

A loving hand serves to give your child comfort and security. It can be quite useful for a big hug! It can bring a bright smile when used for ruffling curly hair, or pulling a pigtail!

Children like to be loved, to be touched. **MAKE YOURS A HELPING HAND AND A LOVING ONE.**

(This does not mean we never punish!)

THE BOWDOIN METHOD

Tell Your Child *Why*

Explain to your child why he can or cannot do something. This will help him build good feelings.

When we set limits to his behavior, we may say such things as:

"No. I'm sorry, but we do not do that."

"I cannot let you hurt Johnny."

"I love you, but not the way you're acting."

Our children need the security of knowing that they cannot do just as they please — and *why*:

"You can't go into the street. It isn't safe."

"You cannot hurt the baby. She is little."

"You cannot mess up the table. I would have to clean it up."

"You cannot run in this room. You might break the lamp."

Accept Your Child's Feelings

"I hurted my finger, Mommy." And your child begins to cry.

So you say, "Hush—you're not hurt."

What usually happens then? Well, the child gets louder and louder and says, "I *am* too! I hurted it."

Try something different. Accept the fact that your child did, indeed, hurt his finger—even though you know better. It may keep down trouble.

The conversation, then, may go like this:
"I hurted my finger, Mommy." (He starts to cry.)

"Yes. I know it hurts. Come let me see it." (Child stops crying.)

"Mommy, put something on it."

"Okay, we'll wash it in cool water." Or, "I'll kiss it and make it well."

It's all over, and your child got the attention he needed. You didn't have to listen to continual crying and whining, and everyone is happier. This works like magic.

Just remember to **accept your child's feelings** without arguing or ridiculing:

"I know how you feel. . . ."

"Sure you're angry, but. . . ."

"I know you don't want Mommy to leave."

Try this method. You will have less trouble at home. Your child will be happier. And you will have less trouble.

Use "I," Not "You"

This approach with children is simple and can be very effective.

Don't say: "**You** didn't clean up your room."
But say: "**I** am not happy because your room is messy."

Not: "**You** know better than to act that way."
But: "**I** am not happy when you act that way."

Not: "**You** are horrible today."
But: "**I** feel bad inside when you cry and whine."

Try to remember to use **"I,"** not **"You"** when you want to change behavior. The idea is that the emphasis is on **your problem** and **not the child's.**

(This idea is used by Dr. Thomas Gordon in his book, *Parent Effectiveness Training*.)

Words Talk!

"You dummy, you—why can't you learn?"

There may be times when these words come out in spite of ourselves. But words talk. They say things.

Sometimes words are warm and comforting. Other times they are cruel and painful.

And our own children believe our words. What we say to them helps them think, and see, and believe. What they believe about themselves is what they become.

Sure we have bad days. Our head aches. We have a fuss with our wife or husband. Money is short and bills pile up. So we take it out on our children.

How sad!

A wise parent will say:

"I am sorry. I feel real bad inside. And I'm taking it out on you. Please forgive me."

You may not agree with this approach, but try it and see. We can, at least, admit to our faults and ask forgiveness. Then we can expect (and we will get) the same from our children.

Tired?

Of course you may be.

And when we get tired, we often take it out on those we love most.

But our children don't understand this.

So we can say to them:

"Mommy is tired. I've had a bad day."

"If you play quietly by yourself and let me rest a bit, perhaps I'll feel better soon."

Try this instead of yelling, fussing, and complaining to your little one. We think it will work for you.

"I Can't Let You Hurt Mary"

A child has to learn how to get along with others and to respect their feelings and rights.

Your child may need to be helped to understand that he cannot hurt others:

"No! We do **not** hurt Mary."

This is very firm, but polite. To find that there are limits to what he can do will give your child a secure feeling.

If your child continues to bite, kick, pinch, pull hair, or hit, he may be trying to tell you something about a problem he has. Although he is unable to tell you in words, he may be behaving this way to tell you that he is jealous or troubled and unable to do well.

Listen parents. Your child may be trying to speak through his behavior. But as you're trying to find and deal with his problem, you will still need to step in and prevent him from hurting others.

You may need only to say, "I won't let you do that—it hurts." If your child throws an object, take it away.

PAGE 216

THE BOWDOIN METHOD

"Don't Be A Baby!"

"Don't be a baby," you may say, "You know you aren't afraid."

Oh, but he may be! And shaming won't help.

Children are afraid of many things: loud noises, like trucks, thunder, and vacuum cleaners; large objects, such as big trucks, big hats, and sometimes wrinkled or handicapped people, if they have never been around them.

They are afraid of animals, especially dogs—and later on, wild animals. And they fear the dark, policemen, thunder, doctors, and dentists.

They fear the unknown: moving to a new house, separation from mother at bedtime, or seeing father leave. Even experiences such as going to the barbershop can scare children.

Wise parents know these fears are normal. They comfort the child immediately. They allow their youngster to show his fears.

Let him say he is afraid. "I know you're afraid. But I am here with you. I won't let anything hurt you."

Prepare your child in advance for a visit to the dentist or doctor. If it is time for a shot, saying it won't hurt is not being honest. So say, "It will hurt a little, but not for long."

Assure your child that you will be back when you leave him. In time, he will conquer his fears without becoming emotionally harmed.

Let him feel sure of your love and that he is safe at home and at school.

"I Don't Love You Anymore"

A wise parent will never say this to her child.

Although we do not always like our child's behavior, we do love the child.

It is best to let a child know that we love him always and at all times, but we may not like the way he acts sometimes.

In this way he will be secure and feel needed. He will grow up to be a better person. And he will be able to achieve more in school.

Yes, we love the child! We make allowances for mistakes, for they are part of growing up. But we are firm, kind, and consistent about not liking bad behavior.

"Stop, Boy!"

Sometimes our young children call one another "boy" or "girl" instead of using their real names.

Encourage your child to use the real name.

"Sarah, if you want Tommy to stop, say, 'Would you please stop, Tommy?' and I'll bet he will stop."

"If you ask Tommy gently and call his name instead of calling him 'boy,' he will probably stop bothering you. Try it."

This kind of language is exciting for little ones! They feel it is grown-up talk. They will be kind and polite, if we teach them to be. But they need practice and good examples.

"You Heard Me!"

Do you ever say this?

Most of us do when we lose our patience.

Sometimes our young children don't mind or don't listen, and we raise our voices at them.

Dangerous behavior has to be stopped at once. But a lot of troublesome behavior can be stopped when you say things like:

"Come, Johnny, play with your toy."

"Jane, help me fold the clothes."

"You're tired, Jill. Get in my lap and I'll read you a book."

"Big Boys Don't Cry"

But boys and girls of all sizes cry. It's all very natural. And we should not try to shame their tears away.

It's far better to say something sympathetic:

"Yes, dear, I know it hurts."

"I would cry, too, if that happened to me."

We need to realize that a little one often cries when things don't go his way or when he needs to get our attention. When we think this is happening, we can get his mind off himself by letting him cry a little while. Then we can say, "Look at this nice book," or "Will you help me with this?"

Soon he will forget what was bothering him.

The Misbehaving Child

Often when a child keeps misbehaving it's because he needs attention. He wants to be noticed. When we think this is happening, we should try to find something good and compliment him.

Sometimes a compliment for something nice, or an extra hug, or a pat on the back will give him the attention he needs. This may head off bad behavior.

All behavior has a cause. When a child misbehaves often, he may be saying, "I need somebody to notice me."

This doesn't mean we shouldn't set limits on his behavior. But if we can see the real cause, we can prevent a lot of behavior problems from happening.

The Lonely Child

Some children have trouble making friends. These are usually children who will grow up to be unhappy unless they're helped.

What can we do when our child is still young that will help him make friends easily? Here are some things:

1. Talk to him about being nice and kind to other children.

2. Invite other children to play with him.

3. Help him learn to speak kindly to others.

4. Encourage him to share his play things.

5. Teach him that he has to be a friend to get a friend.

6. Teach him to use polite words.

Children who make friends easily have less trouble in school. The **first five years** is the time to build a foundation of friendliness. **Make these years count.**

The Cross Child

There are days when children are naturally cross. It happens to all children when they are tired, sleepy, or feeling a little sick.

"Well, what in the world is wrong with you? You sure are a bad girl." Saying this is *not* the way to help your child.

A wise parent will, of course, have understanding and show it: "I know you feel bad on the inside. I feel bad sometimes, too."

Just the fact that you sympathize with your child and understand there are reasons for his behavior will make him feel more secure and not act cross.

Another way to get his mind off his bad feelings—if he isn't feeling **too** bad—is just to invite him to help you work around the house.

And reading or telling him a story can be magic medicine!

The Child With Nervous Habits

If your child sucks his thumb, bites his nails, or twists his hair, he is showing that he may be nervous.

Thumb-sucking is extremely common in babies. Most people today do not believe it will change the shape of the mouth — unless it continues after the second teeth appear.

But if your child continues to suck his thumb after he begins school, or if he bites his nails or twists his hair, he is probably under some kind of emotional strain. He is doing this for some reason.

Tying his hands or nagging him about it won't help.

It's clear he is trying to comfort himself in his own way.

What can you do?

Don't scold or threaten. It will take patience and understanding to help him overcome his habits. Consider the following methods:

1. Maybe he needs to be around other children and make more friends.

2. Look for simple ways to make his life more satisfying.

3. Try to find out if he feels jealous of an older or younger child in the family. (This is hard to do.)

4. Maybe he needs to be given a chance of doing things for himself.

5. Try to decide if you're being too hard on him or expecting too much from him.

Work with his teachers in trying to find the causes of his behavior. Have a little heart-to-heart talk with his teacher. You may even work out a signal to remind him of his habit so that other family members or schoolmates won't know about. (He may even like this little secret!)

The Shy Child

You may get worried when your child hides his head under your skirt if a stranger comes to the door... or when you want your child to talk, and he won't... or when he hides from company... or when he won't stay around other children.

Some timid acts are just a part of growing up. But some indicate severe cases that need help.

Begin now, if your child seems very shy. Help him have friends. Invite children over to play with him.

Avoid constant fault-finding and criticism. Teach him to do things for himself and praise him when he does. Get to the problem before it becomes too serious.

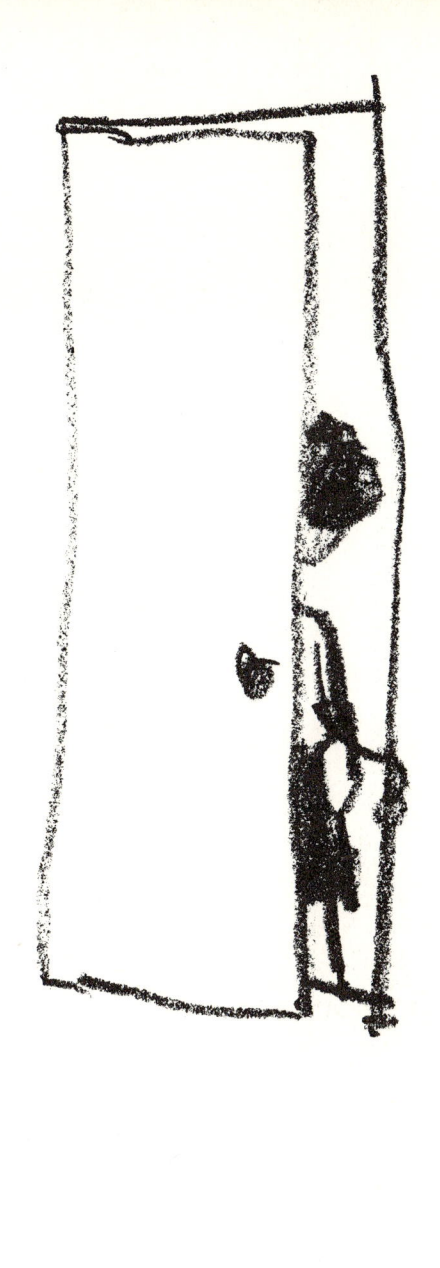

The Overly-Dependent Child

"Ma!... Ma...!"

Does your child want to be with you all the time? Is he insecure when you're not around? Does he cry when you leave?

If he does any of these things often, he may be fearful or anxious. He may need more signs of approval from you. Providing opportunities for other children to play with him may help give the security he needs.

When you leave, assure him that you will be back. Tell him that you will be near if he needs you.

Try to provide a happy home.

Your child needs to let go of you. And sometimes you need to let go of him to keep him from being too dependent on you.

The Stuttering Child

"Mary, I said tell me. Don't just stand there and say 'I . . . I . . . I.' Hurry up! Now say it again. You know you can talk, but you're not trying."

This mother is causing her child's problem to be a bigger one. Many children go through the stage of stuttering and stammering between the ages of two and five. It is best to ignore it and not call it to their attention.

A child may begin to stutter when he enters school, because this is a big adjustment to him.

Stuttering usually means that the child is under too much nervous tension.

If he has had a severe emotional shock, he may start to stutter. Stuttering is sometimes caused by our trying to make our child stop thumb-sucking or nail-biting.

Trying to force a left-handed child to use his right hand may also cause stuttering. At the age of two, a child usually uses both of his hands equally. Let him decide which hand he wants to use.

If your child stutters, ease the tension on him and ask his teacher to try to get you some professional help.

Don't Expect Your Child To Be An Angel

He can't. She can't. Children will naturally do some things sometimes which will bother you.

But children need to be children—not little adults. There are times when we can expect our children to misbehave. When they are sleepy, sick, or fretful they are likely to do things which do not please us.

If we understand that his is normal for our children, it will help us accept them and sympathize with them when they have their problems.

It is often wise to ignore little things, rather than make a big issue over them.

None of us is perfect!

PARENT ACTIVITIES FOR
HOW TO MANAGE YOUR CHILD FOR GOOD BEHAVIOR

Read each statement. Circle yes if you agree and no if you do not agree.

Yes No 1. Children actually want discipline.
Yes No 2. Lonely children need more time by themselves.
Yes No 3. If your child does not want you to leave home, it is advisable to "slip off" without telling.
Yes No 4. When it comes to disciplining my child, I should not ignore any bad behavior.
Yes No 5. It is wise to give my child everything in the right hand and he/she will not be left-handed.
Yes No 6. If your child gets what he wants he/she will learn to "handle" you.
Yes No 7. It is good to praise your child even when it is not deserved.
Yes No 8. Being too easy or being too hard on my child is not good.
Yes No 9. It is often good for children when we parents admit our faults or ask forgiveness.
Yes No 10. "You know you aren't afraid" are good words to say.

Did you have 6 no and 4 yes? If not, answers may be found on pages 206, 221, 225, 227, 226, 210, 206, 207, 214 and 217.

Complete the blanks:

Wise parents know that some fears are normal for little children. List a few things you may do to help your children conquer their fears. (If you need help, review page 217)

1._____
2._____
3._____
4._____
5._____

A little attention may head off bad behavior. We can do this by giving children:

1._____
2._____   *(See page 220, add any others.)*
3._____

If it seems that your child is developing shy behavior, you may do the following:

1._____
2._____
3._____   *(See page 224)*
4._____

Children who are polite are better accepted and seem to be happier and have more friends. What are some polite things you are teaching your child to say to others?

_____
_____

(refer to page 209 and add your own)

Think about your own child. If your child is inclined to be lonely, which of the six things listed on page 221 would you feel you need to do for *your own child*? You are already doing some of these. Write only the numbers of those you wish to try.

( )   ( )   ( )   ( )   ( )   ( )

* * * * * * * * * *

The most important things which help parents in managing behavior without fussing or nagging are:
1. Be c _ _ _ _ _ _ _ _ _
2. Be k _ _ _ but f _ _ _ _.
3. Don't f _ _ _ or n _ _.
4. Set l _ _ _ _ _ on behavior.
5. Be a good e _ _ _ _ _ _ _.
6. Without arguing or ridiculing, accept your child's f _ _ _ _ _ _ _.
7. Teach your child s _ _ _ c _ _ _ _ _ _.

(Check pages 206, 207, 211 and 212)

* * * * * * * * *

Here are some examples of behavior which you may expect of children. There are two acceptable ways of handling this behavior. Place a (1) in the space which shows the "best" way; place (2) in the space which you consider the "next best."

Your child is running in the house. This is not acceptable to you.
    ( ) "I'll whip you if you do that!"
    ( ) "Stop running immediately!"
    ( ) "Good girls don't run in the house."
    ( ) "No running! Outside is the place for running, besides the baby is sleeping."

(See page 211)

* * * * * * * * *

Your child left toys on the floor. You want to change this behavior.
    ( ) "I'm going to write Granny not to buy you any more toys until you learn to pick them up."
    ( ) "I am not happy because your toys are on the floor." (Point to the toys and wait.)
    ( ) "You sure are messy. Wait until your father sees this!"
    ( ) "You must pick up your toys. Come, I'll help you get started."

(See page 213)

* * * * * * * * *

Your child has been told many times not to throw an object but he/she throws it anyway.
    ( ) "Sorry but I'll have to put away your blocks. *No more playing* with them."
    ( ) "You will have to go to bed."
    ( ) Hold your child's hand and say firmly "You *cannot* do that!"
    ( ) "Aren't you ashamed of yourself?"

(See page 216)

* * * * * * * * *

Four year old Sally has hurt her toe. It isn't badly hurt but she keeps crying.
    ( ) "I didn't know you were such a cry baby!"
    ( ) "Come and let's put your doll on some clean clothes."
    ( ) "It makes me ashamed of you to see you cry!"
    ( ) "I know it hurts. Come and let me hold you!"

(See page 219 and 212)

* * * * * * * * *

These are everyday problems that parents face. If you think the parent handled it well, write "wise" in the blank provided; if not, write "unwise". Fill in each blank.

Your four year old tells a "tale" that you know is not true, such as "I saw a big animal with fire coming out of its mouth!"

THE BOWDOIN METHOD

_____ Parent: "That's a scary story, but of course it isn't true!"

_____ Parent: "You know you are telling a lie. It's bad to lie like that!"

_____ Parent: "You are a bad boy to make up such a wild story!"

_____ Parent: "That is a "make believe" story. Some stories are true and some are "make believe"! Sometime I'll tell you a make-believe story!"

(Did you have two wise, two unwise?)

Remember: Young children have to learn to distinguish fact from fiction without being called a liar.

Mary and Jean are playing. They are five years old. Mary slightly pushes Jean, obviously not hurting her. Jean cries as if she has been "half-killed" and runs to tell her parent.

_____ Parent: "Let me see where it hurts. (looks) I don't see any bruises. It must not hurt much!"

_____ Parent: "You tell Mary I want to see her this minute! I'll make her sorry for hurting you!"

_____ Parent: "Mary didn't mean to hurt you, I'm sure. She likes you. She's just playing."

_____ Parent: "Mary, don't you be pushing Jean and I mean it!"

(Did you have two wise, two unwise parents?)

Remember: It is best to discourage "tattling" by not making a big issue of it, unless the child were really hurt! To make a big thing of it only encourages the child to "tattle" more for the attention it gives.

Four year old Carlos and John are playing when suddenly John does not get his way and starts hitting and fighting Carlos. In handling this situation which parents are wise or unwise?

_____ Parent: "You *cannot* do that! I cannot let you hit Carlos!
(Parent stops the behavior immediately).

_____ Parent: "I'm ashamed of both of you. I thought you both were nice boys but you aren't!"

_____ Parent: "That hurts! If you cannot play nicely together, you can't play at all. Just one more time like this and you will have to go to your room, John."

_____ Parent: "You just wait, John; I'll tell your father when he comes home and he'll take care of you."

(Did you have two wise and two unwise parents?)

Remember: Shame breeds guilt and guilt at this age isn't good. Neither should father be used as a threat!)

* * * * * * * * * *

You as a parent often are tired and you may be cross. Your children don't always understand when you have problems. You will have more harmony in the home if you do either of *three things*. Place a mark in each of the three places.

(   ) Parent: "I am sorry. I don't feel well and I'm taking it out on you."

(   ) Parent: "You are simply driving me crazy!"

(   ) Parent: "I know how you feel when I'm so cross. Please forgive me."

(   ) Parent: "I am tired and I've had a bad day at work. Please understand I'm not mad at you. Thank you for helping me!"

* * * * * * * * * *

Sam is not the oldest child at home but he is five years old and is the biggest. He never plays for more than a few minutes without bothering the other children. He snatches toys, pulls hair, bites. He has a problem that may have many causes. What do you think some of these could be?
(Review the book for suggestions).

_____

_____

* * * * * * * * *

Read this episode of Ellen and her mother. In the spaces provided list the wise and unwise things which occured.

          (Mother is inside. Ellen, her 3½ year old is outside playing in the yard.)

MOTHER: (in a loud voice) Ellen stop playing and come in this house this minute!

ELLEN: No. Me want to play.

MOTHER: You heard me, "girl"!

ELLEN: I played till supper last time!

MOTHER: Yesterday was another day and that's my business young lady!

    (Mother comes out with a ruler and threatens Ellen who comes in crying).

MOTHER: I don't know what I'm going to do with you. You are horrible today!
(Ellen continues to cry.)
And stop that crying! Stop it I said! (Shakes her)

    (Finally Ellen stops crying and mother tries to change her mood).

MOTHER: I'll tell you what let's do. Come, help me fold the clothes. You may fold the little things. (Mother picks up a washcloth to show her.)

My! You are a good helper. I'm proud of you! I must remember to tell daddy what a big girl you are!

ELLEN: Daddy likes me!

MOTHER: But he doesn't like you when you're bad!
(Ellen trips over chair and overruns clothes that had been placed there).

MOTHER: How CAN you be so clumsy? Look what a problem you cause me... now I'll have to pick them all up!

ELLEN: Me pick up too.

MOTHER: No, you're too little! Besides, you'll just mess up again!
(Ellen almost cries, but mother tries to "collect" herself).

I'll read you a pretty book when we get finished. That'll be fun! Reading is fun!

         * * * * * * * * *

Wise Things Mother Did	**Unwise Things Mother Did**
1._____	1._____
2._____	2._____
3._____	3._____
4._____	4._____
5._____	5._____
6._____	6._____

(You should have four to six things in each category.)

THE BOWDOIN METHOD

NOTES

NOTES

NOTES

NOTES

NOTES

NOTES

NOTES

NOTES

NOTES